PRETTY DEAD

VICTORIA MATTSEN CRIME SERIES
BOOK 5

IFEANYI ESIMAI

eISBN: 978-1-63589-799-9
Print ISBN: 978-1-63589-800-2
Audio ISBN: 978-1-63589-801-9
Cover design www.coveredbymelinda.com

Published by
ShotReads, an imprint of
Ciparum LLC
270 Sparta Ave., Suite 104, PMB 152
Sparta, NJ 07871

Get a FREE copy of The Rookie! - scan the QR code or visit
www.ifeanyiEsimai.com

For Chinwe...Always.
The wind beneath my wings.

ACKNOWLEDGMENTS

My heartfelt gratitude goes out to my family and friends, whose unwavering faith in me fueled this project from the very start.

I also want to extend a special thanks to a group of incredible individuals whose generous spirit has made an indelible impact on this project, and for that, I am forever grateful.

Erik S
Nneka Anaebonam
Craig Martelle
Jenn Davidson
Chinwe Anyamele
Obioha Emezie
Renee
Okechukwu Obua
Romeo Richards
Ikenna Emeghara
Charles Onunkwo
Adaeze

Every one of you has helped shape this journey in your own unique way, and I couldn't be more thankful. Your support has not only made these books a reality but has also inspired me as I continue to tell Detective Vikki Mattsen's story.

To all the readers, thank you for inviting Detective Vikki

Mattsen into your lives. It's been a joy to share this adventure with you.

Here's to the stories yet to be told.

PROLOGUE

Beauty queens seemed to fade into oblivion—it never crossed Paige Arden's mind that missing queens turned into dead girls. You couldn't become Miss America without participating in the process. Nor win the Power Ball jackpot without buying a ticket—Paige Arden wanted it all.

First, she needed a portfolio from a well-known photographer. She'd heard about small-town beauty queens hitting it big. Going to New York for a photo shoot had opened her eyes to the possibilities. It could be her.

At the studio, she saw girls living the life she imagined for herself down the road. They wore the best fashion designer outfits, Rolex watches, expensive jewelry, and rich boyfriends at their beck and call. The smell of success was in the air, and Paige inhaled much of it.

She could win Miss Sussex County, Miss New Jersey, then the coveted prize of all, Miss America.

"But you have to go for it," Mark said while he snapped away with his Nikon. The mechanical double-shutter sound of the camera filled the air. "Pout your lips for me, honey."

The camera made the now familiar whining sound.

"Beautiful! You are a natural."

Snap. Snap.

"Make a face like you just tasted the best cheeseburger ever." Mark laughed. "I know you don't eat fast food."

The camera whined.

"Yes!"

That was Saturday.

Sunday evening, Paige scanned her room in her small apartment and thought of the future.

As the reigning queen of St. Ives Beauty & Brains Pageant, she'd already seen firsthand the attention it brought. Men who were way above her pay grade suddenly noticed her. She'd showed up like a shooting star.

And most of all, they all wanted her. For the first time in her life, she could choose what she wanted and not be forced by circumstance.

She stood in front of her closet, took a deep breath, and blew it out. "Paige, what would it be?"

Her iPhone rang. She removed the blanket and reached for it on her nightstand. It was her mother, and she'd called a few times. Paige unplugged it from the charger.

"Hi, Mom."

"Paige! About time. I've been trying to get hold of you. How was New York?"

"Great but exhausting. I've been sleeping all day. I didn't know photo shoots were this demanding!"

"Well, that's life," her mother said. "Contrary to what people say, the best things in life are not free. You have to work for them. I'm glad you had fun. You took plenty of pictures?"

"Oh my God—a lot. Mark said I have the looks to go far in the industry. It was all up to me."

Her mother paused. "And Mark is...?"

"The photographer. But it would take a lot of commit-ment, especially since I love my day job at the school, too."

"I was going to ask you about that," her mom said. "Well, you have time to think about it. We'll talk some more when you come over."

A glance at the wall clock told Paige she'd better get out of bed, shower, and get ready for her date.

Paige was in and out of the bathroom. She'd shampooed her hair and dried it. The shower was a good place to think. Now she had a better idea of what to do between her day job and becoming a super beauty queen.

Tonight she'd wear something simple. It was only dinner. A pair of distressed jeans and a black blouse. Cat-eye makeup and a light skin-tone foundation.

She slipped on her underthings and her clothes. Paige hadn't worn her cowboy boots in a while. She wore a pair of cotton socks and was about to put on her boot when there was a knock on her door.

Paige checked the time. She wasn't late yet. She walked to the door and looked through the peephole. Her lips parted in a smile. She removed the security chain, unlocked and opened the door.

She cocked her head and smiled. "Hey, you. Come in." Paige turned and headed for her room. Behind her, the door clicked shut, and the lock turned. She reached for her cowboy boots.

"This is CNN." The sound came from the TV.

Paige giggled. "Make yourself at home while I get into these boots. I have some juice in the fridge if you're interested."

She sat on her bed, her back to the door, and bent down to pull up the boot while she forced her foot down. One foot was in. Paige was working on getting the second boot in when she felt a presence behind her.

She glanced over her shoulder. "You came to help? I'm almost done. One leg to go."

Paige's blouse tail must have ridden up because she felt a cold, clammy hand on her waist.

She whirled. "What are you—?"

The fist caught her on the jaw—propelled her forward. Pain exploded in her head. She fell, landing on her side.

Paige got on her hands and knees. She tasted blood. "Oh my God... Why?" She sounded funny. Blood dripped from her mouth like the first raindrops before a downpour.

The kicks came in a relentless torrent. Her face, stomach, thighs, head— all were pummeled. A veil of darkness shrouded her before the world faded away.

CHAPTER ONE

Homicide Detective Victoria Mattsen, Vikki for short, stood in line at the coffee shop. The smell of java, freshly baked croissants, bacon, and eggs forced saliva into her mouth. She swallowed, hoping the line would move faster.

Three people were in front of her. The cashier repeated the order of the person she was attending to. "Medium French vanilla coffee, black. Egg and cheese on a buttered English muffin. Do you want it toasted? That will be…"

Vikki tuned out. She was dressed in a black pantsuit and black blouse. She subconsciously tugged down at her suit to make sure it hid her holstered Glock 19. She wondered what this week would be like at work.

She'd come a long way from her early twenties when she'd joined the police force. The murder of her friend, Alexis, and her dad, Mike Devoe, made her decide to join the police. On her first week as a rookie, an encounter with some criminals changed her life. She'd done things she ordinarily wouldn't have done for the next ten years.

"I didn't know I was going to meet you here," said a familiar voice behind her.

She knew that voice. A tingle ran down her spine. Vikki smiled and turned. "Good morning, Dr. Brandon. There are no coincidences in life. If it were someone else, I would have believed that."

Dressed in blue scrubs, he smiled and folded his hands over his chest, showing off bulging biceps. "No, I just stopped for coffee. I noticed the white Explorer, but there's no way I would have known it was yours."

"How can I help you?" said the cashier.

Vikki placed her order and went to the pickup section. Dr. Brandon joined her a few minutes later.

"How's your evening looking?"

"I get off around five, six, or seven...depending."

"Wow, that sounds like you might end up sleeping at work. What about we get dinner together? Do you like Chinese food? I know this place that has the best Chinese cuisine ever."

Before Vikki could second-guess herself, she said, "Why not."

Dr. Brandon smiled. "I'll text you the address. It's a date."

Heat rushed to Vikki's cheeks. She nodded.

"Victoria!" one of the baristas called out.

Vikki picked up her food and left. She felt his eyes on her back as heat.

She got in her car and headed toward the police department when her cell phone rang. She looked at the screen. It was Jody, the police department's admin.

Jody was sixty-five and widowed. SIPD and her cats were all the family she wanted and needed to keep going. Jody had been at the office longer than everyone else and knew where the bones were buried. She was the person to talk to if you had questions about the police department or needed favors.

"Hello, Jody."

"Vikki, I hope I caught you at a good time. We got a call

from St. Martins Academy. One of their teachers failed to show up for class this morning."

"Maybe she took a personal day."

"That's what I said, too. But they said she's dedicated to her students and wouldn't leave them hanging. She's also the current reigning Miss St. Ives Beauty and Brains Pageant."

"Text me the address. I'll head over there. Could you let Gomez know, too?"

"He might get there before you. I called him first out of habit."

"That's fine. Talk later." Vikki hung up. A beauty queen and a teacher. Vikki hoped it was nothing. Hoping she'd slept in or had an errand to run. But, from her experience, when people were worried enough to call the police, most of the time, they were right.

CHAPTER TWO

At nine-thirty a.m., Vikki drove her white Ford Explorer into the parking lot of the victim's apartment complex—her heart sank. Four police cruisers were stationed in front of the building with strobe lights flashing. That could only mean bad news.

Vikki attached her badge to a lanyard and hung it around her neck. She stepped out of her car and scrutinized the small crowd in front of the building. Vikki brought out her phone and shot a video of them. Sometimes the perp returned to gloat over their handiwork.

She approached the entrance and turned the doorknob. Locked. "Christ." One of those doors. Either you knew the combination or had to be buzzed in if you didn't live there.

On her right on the wall was a panel with numbers and buttons. She pushed the button for 302. Jody had texted her the number. The uniform there would probably ignore it.

She waited a moment, then contemplated pushing all the buttons, hoping one of the tenants would buzz her in, thinking it was the mailman. A movement inside caught her eye.

A man approached the door, eyebrows raised.

Vikki untangled her ring pendant necklace from the lanyard of her shield and pressed her badge against the glass door. The man walked faster and opened the door.

"Morning. I'm Bill Scott, the apartment manager." He was middle-aged, bald, with a considerable girth.

Vikki stepped in. "Thanks. I'm Detective Victoria Mattsen, SIPD."

They shook hands.

"I thought I'd be here to help the police get in and out of the building," Bill Scott said. "I'm still in shock."

Vikki nodded. She took in the foyer with locked pigeon-hole mailboxes on one wall. The place smelled of new carpet, coffee, and garbage. She headed for the elevator door on the wall to her right.

Vikki pointed at a white camera screwed into the wall. "Does this work?"

Bill Scott shook his head. "No, it's a dummy. A deterrent. Now, I wish we'd installed the real thing."

Vikki offered him her card. "Please call if you remember anything."

Bill Scott fumbled in his pocket and offered Vikki a card. "Reciprocity."

Vikki rode the elevator to the third floor. She stepped out and followed the sign on the wall indicating which way to go. The closer she got to the apartment, the more the air smelled like iron syrup.

An officer standing in front of the apartment smiled and gave her a logbook.

"Thank you." Vikki signed and handed it back. She ducked under the yellow police tape and stepped in.

The door led into the living room. On the right was the dining area and the kitchen.

A modeling and beauty pageant magazine on the coffee

table in the living room got her attention. The open magazine on top, a modeling piece was dog-eared—a destination photo shoot opportunity.

Had she been thinking of a modeling gig? Peeking out from underneath the magazine was a math textbook. Math and modeling?

Facing the coffee table was a three-seater leather couch propped up against the wall. The dining area was a mini round table with three chairs. A laptop was open on it.

A man and woman in CSU vests walked methodically, dusting for fingerprints and collecting fibers. A piece of the carpet was cut off and bagged.

Vikki hadn't seen any signs of struggle. Voices came from a room to her right, and she headed in that direction.

"Runway!"

"It was Mike Gomez, her partner since she'd joined SIPD. He was on track to retire in a couple of years and planned to sail the world with his wife after. With every homicide case that came their way, he ensured that Vikki was the lead detective.

"This is right up your alley," Gomez said. "Models and beauty queens."

Vikki, many years ago, as a college student in Paris, had done some modeling on the side. Her friends at the police academy had found out and baptized her Runway. The name hadn't stuck, but now and then, someone threw it out.

She ignored Gomez's remarks and went straight to business. "What do we have?"

Gomez shook his head and waved her over to the side of the bed. "It's brutal."

Vikki caught sight of the bedroom wall and froze. It could pass as a canvas for the beginning of a Jackson Pollock color spatter done in dark red. The smell of blood plus a sweet fruity-rosy smell like raspberry was overpowering. Vikki glanced around for a dish of fruits or roses in a vase. Found none. She focused on the victim.

"The victim is Paige Arden, twenty-two years old. A high school math teacher at St. Martins Academy. And also the reigning Miss St. Ives Beauty and Brains."

Vikki remembered the math textbook with the modeling magazines and understood. Paige Arden had two passions.

"I think the perp came in from the living room and attacked her. She was probably knocked out, stabbed, then strangled."

Vikki hoovered over the naked blood-smeared form of Paige Arden. She lay on her back, blue eyes glazed over, staring into space, not seeing. One sock remained on her left foot, the other wrapped around her neck. Her torso, abdomen—all over her body were covered in stab wounds. They looked like someone had drawn short straight lines on her with a permanent marker.

Her left shoulder was raised. Vikki went closer. They stooped down and caught a glimpse of the handle of a knife. The blade was probably buried deep in her back.

A pair of cowboy boots lay on each side of the foot of the bed. One foot was splattered with blood. Her jeans, blouse, panties, and bra were strewn across the floor.

Vikki swallowed. She had seen a lot of gruesome since becoming a homicide dick. But this was one of the worst. It reminded her of another scene twelve years ago when she'd returned home on St. Patrick's Day and met a similar situation. Her best friend, Alexis, lay brutalized.

Then she couldn't do anything, but now she had the skills to do something for Paige Arden. Vikki vowed to herself—whoever had done this must face justice.

"What's your theory?" Gomez asked.

"I think she knew the perp. There's no sign of forced entry. She must have let the person in. Somehow, things got out of control and ended in carnage." Vikki glanced around. "Who found her?"

Gomez gestured toward the opposite side of the apartment. A brunette in her early twenties dabbed her eyes with a tissue and talked to a uniform. Vikki wondered how she'd missed her when she'd walked in.

"She's a teacher at the same academy. She and the vic had been friends since high school. Went to Rutgers University together, too. She was worried when Paige didn't show up for her lecture this morning and wouldn't answer her phone. After her first class, she drove up here to check on her."

Vikki headed for the brunette. "I'll ask the uniform to get her to an interview room at the station. We'll get to her as soon as we talk to CSU." From the corner of her eye, she caught the familiar figure of the medical examiner in CSO coming in through the door with his assistants.

She would give him a few minutes to get acquainted with the victim. Then she'd talk to him.

CHAPTER THREE

Jessica Mills was still in shock when Vikki introduced herself to her. She'd go into sudden bursts of sobs and could barely hold a conversation. Vikki felt she needed to leave the crime scene, but she declined to be taken to the hospital.

"I'll have a uniform take you to the police station," Vikki said.

Ms. Mills nodded, and Vikki handed her to one of the uniforms.

Gomez took over his duties. "I'll knock on some neighbor's doors," he said. "Find out what they heard, saw, or felt."

A familiar deep baritone voice doled out instructions. The voice belonged to Dennis Mallory, head of SPIDs CSU. He was meticulous and thorough, and Vikki couldn't wait to hear his theory on what had happened.

About an hour after seeing the ME and his team come in, Vikki returned to the bedroom. Dr. Brandon had a protective apron over his button-down blue shirt and khaki pants and smiled subtly when Vikki walked in.

He was already set up taking pictures. The mechanical double-shutter sound of his Canon camera filled the bedroom. He took many photos of the scene, two from every angle. The blood spatter on the wall also attracted him. The camera purred away.

Vikki watched Brandon snap on gloves, pick up a scalpel, and get down on his knees. She knew what came next and went to the living room. She couldn't bear to see one more incision made on a body ravaged with many. Vikki thought of Brandon's process. Make an incision in her abdomen and insert a thermometer into her liver to get her core temperature.

She scanned Paige's pictures in the living room to keep her mind at ease. They brought back too many memories from her own life. There were pictures from modeling gigs at different locations and during pageants. Paige was pretty and photogenic. She had a lovely smile. Vikki wondered if being a beauty queen had anything to do with what had happened here.

She wished it hadn't happened, just like she always thought it would have made a difference if she had been home the day Alexis and her dad had been murdered.

"Detective Mattsen."

It was Dr. Brandon. He waved her over. This time there was no smile. He was all serious—all business.

"Based on temperature and lividity, death occurred between seven and nine p.m. Before you ask, I don't know what caused her death until I get her back to the lab and order some tests." He gestured at the body. "But your guess is as good as mine. Whoever did this is emotionally bankrupt."

Vikki nodded. The technicians with him opened a black body bag next to the victim.

"I have to go. I'll let you know once I find something."

It was Vikki's cue to walk away. She wandered back to the living room, not wanting to see them lift Paige and put her in the body bag. They'd done the same for Alexis, and she'd watched it all. She hoped Gomez found something knocking on doors. She couldn't wait to talk to Jessica Mills, too. Hopefully, she had an idea of what had happened.

Gomez walked back in, shaking his head. "Most of the tenants didn't answer the door. Considering it's Monday morning. The two who answered were not home Sunday night."

Vikki inhaled and blew it out. "Well, come back, or send uniforms to interview the neighbors. The ME placed the time of death between seven and nine p.m. Sunday."

"Gomez. Mattsen."

It was Mallory.

"We have an idea of what happened here," Mallory said. "If you can, come over here."

CHAPTER FOUR

Mallory did not waste any time. Before joining the crime scene unit, he had been in the trenches for more than fifteen years as a homicide detective. He knew the importance of gathering evidence the proper way.

"I think the victim knew the perp," Mallory said. "Or at least she wasn't threatened by their presence. There are no signs of forced entry." He opened the door to Paige Arden's apartment and ran his gloved hand along both sides of the door, showing they hadn't been tampered with.

Gomez glanced at the window.

Mallory shook his head. "Her apartment is on the third floor. It's a new building. No added fire escape after the fact. Unless the perp is a cousin to Spider-Man, there's no way they could have climbed up."

Vikki nodded.

Mallory continued. "She must have turned her back on him and walked to the bedroom."

Vikki raised an eyebrow. "Him?"

"Him, yes, because of what happened next. She must have turned her back on him. There are no defensive wounds on her. It was a total surprise for the victim. If she were facing him and saw his fist coming up, she would have raised her hand or done something to protect herself. He proceeded to punch and kick her, incapacitating her. He removed her clothes and raped her."

Vikki's inside tightened.

Mallory paused to make sure they were all on the same page. "He's done, and clarity comes. She's on the floor whimpering. Maybe something triggered the attack. Or he came with a plan—she knows him. He can't leave her alive. He goes to the kitchen, gets a knife, and stabs her repeatedly. But she doesn't die. Or she's dead, and air escapes her lungs as a moan. He pulls off one sock from her leg and strangles her."

"That is wicked," Gomez said, face flushed. "We'll nail the bastard."

There was silence.

Vikki raised her head. "He must have left DNA. All that stabbing. He could have cut himself in the process."

"You're right," Mallory said. "He could have. But we don't know for sure. All the blood will be matched and typed. His outfit must have been covered in blood."

"I mean with the rape," Vikki said.

"We don't know for sure. The ME will have a rape kit done, and the result will guide our actions. But we found a piece of a condom wrapper. We'll dust that for prints and DNA."

Vikki let out a breath. That news made her feel a little better. There was hope.

Mallory sighed. "We have lifted a few fingerprints, but places we expected them to be like the doorknobs, he had to let himself out. The knife—were all wiped down. Her purse with two hundred dollars in it was on her dresser. So we don't think robbery was a motive here."

Gomez exhaled, anger plastered on his face like clouds of

an approaching thunderstorm. "The sooner we start, the better. We'll have to notify next of kin."

"But, we have Jessica Mills waiting at the station. Let's go talk to her."

CHAPTER FIVE

Vikki arrived at the police department and parked in her usual spot. The weather was overcast, but now it was raining. She stayed in her car, waiting for the rain to abate. The time on her dashboard was noon. The last thing she wanted was to be drenched to the bone before she made it to the building.

A shadow loomed outside her window. Vikki jumped. Why was she so apprehensive? The figure knocked on the glass. It was Gomez, and he had an umbrella.

"Thank God," Vikki muttered. She picked up her handbag, opened the door, and stepped out. "My knight in shining armor."

"Save that for Dr. Brandon. Come on, let's go. This umbrella was built for one person, so stick close."

Rain splashed on her from the car. The air smelled fresh and clean, as if nature was working hard to erase the carnage they'd seen at apartment 302.

The rain stopped once they got to the stairs of the department.

"Typical," Vikki said. She walked up the stairs and into the building.

"Morning again, Vikki," Jody said. She glanced around, then leaned in conspiratorially. "I heard it was brutal."

Vikki pursed her lips and nodded.

"Oh, what a shame, what a shame," Jody said. "She was beautiful and so full of life."

Gomez came in, shaking the umbrella.

Vikki took a step back. "Careful. You didn't help me outside only to drench me indoors."

"Sorry, I wasn't thinking." Gomez wrapped the Velcro sling around the umbrella. "We'll notify Paige's parents once we're done with the interview. I'll pull up their address from the DMV database and get coffee and a bottle of water for Jessica. I'll meet you in the interview room." He winked. "I'll be the bad cop."

"If we get to that," Vikki said. "I hope we don't."

Vikki wasn't a fan, but it was a helpful tool. Being aggressive or intimidating to the subject, a bad cop. Or, appearing sympathetic and understanding, good cop. Both eroded the trust when found out. But, there were terrible people out there who didn't play nice and had to be cornered.

Vikki bypassed the detective squad room and headed for interview one. She stopped at the one-way mirror and observed Jessica Mills. She was shaking her head, a painful expression on her face. Vikki's heart went out to her. Losing your best friend is never easy. She'd been there.

Vikki knocked once and went in. "Hello, sorry for keeping you waiting. We had a few things to finish up at the apartment."

Jessica raised her head. Her eyes were bloodshot. "Hi." Her voice was a croak. "Sorry, I still can't believe it. I spoke with her as she drove back from New York and after she got back."

"Do you know why she was in New York?" Vikki asked.

"She went for a photo shoot."

Vikki nodded and glanced at the ceiling to ensure the camera's light was on. It was. "Did she come back with anyone from New York?"

"No, we spoke all the way. There was no indication someone else was in the car."

There was a knock on the door, and Gomez strolled in with two cups of coffee. He handed one cup to Vikki.

"You remember my partner, Detective Mike Gomez? He was at the CS."

Jessica looked at Gomez and attempted a smile.

"Here." Vikki pushed her cup to Jessica.

"Thank you," said Jessica. She took a sip and placed the cup down.

Vikki sat opposite her and Gomez to her left. The good-cop, bad-cop setup was in place.

"Could you tell us what happened his morning?" Gomez said.

CHAPTER SIX

"I didn't see Paige at morning assembly and presumed she was running late," said Jessica. "But after the first period, I noticed she still hadn't arrived. I called her cell. Her phone was off. I thought she was in the building and asked around. No one had seen her. It wasn't like Paige. She never missed class. She loved teaching and her students." A tear rolled down Jessica's cheek. "I knew something must be wrong."

"What did you do?" Vikki said.

"I teach US history...I gave the class something to read and dashed off to her apartment. I called her on my way, and it still went to voice mail. Now I was panicking. Did she fall in the bath? At her apartment, I rode the elevator up."

Gomez raised his hand.

"I was—" Jessica stopped speaking.

"How did you get in?"

"S-somebody was coming out as I approached the door. They held it open for me." Her big eyes were still on Gomez.

Vikki nodded. "What happened next?"

Jessica swallowed. "Paige's door wasn't locked. I touched the handle, and it opened. I called out to her and entered.

There was an awful metallic odor mixed with the smell of bleach. I walked in, calling her name, and knew something was wrong right away."

"How so?" Gomez asked.

"Paige has a pet peeve...if you open something, close it. At least leave it how you found it. I always forget to close the milk bottle, soda bottle, or doors, and she would remind me. She would never leave her door open."

Tears flowed freely down Jessica's face.

Vikki brought out a pocket tissue from her bag and gave it to her.

Jessica, still sobbing, said, "Then I saw her on the floor—naked, blood everywhere."

Vikki touched her hand. "Take your time. Sip some coffee."

Jessica did as she was told.

"I'm so sorry for your loss," Vikki said. "Do you think you can continue?"

Jessica nodded. "I couldn't look at her. I knew I shouldn't touch anything. I exited the apartment and sat on the floor outside her door. I called nine-one-one and was there until the police came." She shook her head and fumbled in her bag. "Why didn't she use this? I only have it because of her." In her hand was a pink rechargeable micro stun gun. "My dad used to take me with him to the gun range as a child. I hated it. And he'd said, why have a weapon in the house you don't know how to use." Her eyes met Vikki's. "Why didn't she use it?"

Vikki nodded. The taser packed a bunch. And learning how to handle a gun was an excellent skill to have. But she had no answer. And didn't want to buy into an argument about guns. The surprise element in the attack was there. She shook her head and kept her mouth shut.

"We went to Rutgers together—been friends since high

school. Paige always wanted to teach. But the glamour of modeling and pageantry called to her."

Vikki smiled. "I can relate to that. Did she model while she was at Rutgers?"

Jessica opened her mouth, then closed it.

Gomez jumped in. "Detective Mattsen used to be a model in Paris." He smiled. "But putting bad guys away called to her."

Vikki ignored his remarks. "Does she get along with everyone in school?"

For the first time, Jessica smiled.

"Yes!" She sniffed and wiped her nose with the back of her hand. "She's popular, especially with the boys. More than a few requested to be transferred to her class after she won Miss St. Ives Beauty and Brains."

"I bet," Gomez muttered. "All those hormones. Did any of the boys stand out? Like, get closer to her than normal?"

Jessica frowned and shook her head. "I don't think so. Our boys are well-behaved."

"Boys today are so dumb," Gomez said. "When I was in high school, you don't tell on your teachers. You eat your cake and keep your mouth shut. Even Newt Gingrich married his high school geometry teacher. They used—"

Vikki kicked him in the chin.

"Ouch!"

A bewildered Jessica said, "I don't follow. What's a newt...? An amphibian?"

Gomez rubbed his chin and chuckled. "It's a type of salamander who likes math. Don't worry about it."

"Anyone you know who would want to harm Paige?" Vikki asked.

Jessica hesitated. "No." Her voice was barely audible.

Vikki leaned forward. "If there's anything you know, tell

us now. No matter how insignificant you think it is. It might be the next piece that completes the puzzle."

"I've seen her argue with her boyfriend." Jessica let out a nervous giggle. "Who doesn't? A perfect relationship is a fairy tale, right?"

Gomez sat up from rubbing his chin. "What's his name?"

Jessica sighed. "Kevin Murdoch, MD. He's a surgeon at Milton Medical Center."

"Relationships can be tough," Vikki said. "Anything else apart from the occasional disagreements?"

Jessica shook her head.

Since they would look at the boyfriend anyway, Vikki let it go for now. "Where were you between seven and nine p.m. on Sunday?"

"At my parents' home. I always visit them on Sunday."

Vikki took Jessica's parents' phone number and address. "All right, Jessica, thank you." She gave Jessica her card. "I'm so sorry for your loss. An officer will take you to your car. Is that okay?"

Jessica nodded.

"If you remember anything, please call," Vikki said and got up.

"I'll make the arrangements," Gomez said and left.

"So, what happens next?" Jessica asked.

Vikki exhaled. "We'll investigate. Ask questions, look at the gathered evidence, and follow the clues."

There was a knock on the door, and Gomez popped in. "Your car's ready."

Vikki escorted Jessica downstairs and handed her over to a uniform. She watched them drive off, then headed to her Ford Explorer.

"Wait for me," Gomez said and hurried after her.

Inside the car, Vikki typed the address to Paige Arden's

parents' home address into her phone, and they set off. "I think she's hiding something about college."

They continued in silence.

Halfway, Gomez howled with laughter like a hyena. "Oh my God. Gen Z—Newt, a type of amphibian."

"Why did you have to bring up Gingrich?"

"It's a fact. He did marry his high schoolteacher, and they had two daughters."

CHAPTER SEVEN

By the time Vikki and Gomez got to Paige Arden's parent's home, the time on her iPhone was three-thirty p.m. The news of their daughter's death had reached them. Vikki kicked herself for not delegating that job.

Their home was a well-kept colonial. Mr. Arden, a middle-aged man dressed in a black V-neck sweater and tan khaki pants, opened the door after they rang the bell. He welcomed them once they identified themselves and ushered them past the staircase into a large den.

People handled tragedy differently. Some cried. Some got very sick, and a few became suicidal. The Ardens wanted to talk. The least Vikki and Gomez could do was spend some time with them.

Framed pictures of two girls as they grew from babies into adulthood lined the walls and shelves. One of the little girls was Paige. Her younger images showed a beautiful, shy young girl.

Mrs. Arden, a manager at a bank in Milton, kept a brave face. She was dressed in a white shirt and black skirt. A matching black suit was draped over a chair in the dining. It looked like she'd planned to go to work before hearing the news. Her eyes were red.

"My Paige as a young child was a self-imposed wallflower. Shy and awkward and would exclude herself from events. Her friends convinced her to participate in Miss Fairground Beauty Pageant in her last year of high school, and she won!"

"My daughter's gone," Mr. Arden cried in a low voice. "Gone. How could someone do this to us?"

Mrs. Arden's eyes filled with tears. Her lips quivered. She was on the brink of breaking down, but she pulled through.

"Paige was so surprised she won. She never knew she was pretty. She didn't believe it when people told her so. That win gave her the confidence she'd lacked. After that, she blossomed, like a butterfly emerging from the chrysalis into something new but the same."

Mr. Arden sat beside her on the couch, sobbing. Each time his wife extolled Paige, a whimper escaped him. Fresh tears poured down his cheeks. Fathers have a special bond with their daughters and sons with their mothers.

Paige's older sister, Fiona, was there, too. She'd come over after she'd heard. She remained quiet. Vikki attributed it to shock.

"She told me about going to New York for a photo shoot," Mrs. Arden said. "She needed new pictures for her portfolio. I spoke with her soon after she finished the shoot. She was full of praises about the people she met."

"Is there anyone you think might want to hurt Paige?" Gomez asked.

For a moment, nobody spoke.

Vikki tried to explain it in another way. "Anyone who wasn't happy that Paige had come out of her shell and was shining?"

Mrs. Arden shook her head. "No, everyone was happy for her. They loved her."

"Do you know her boyfriend, Kevin Murdock?" Gomez asked.

"Oh, poor Kevin. He'll be heartbroken. They were so much in love," Mrs. Arden said.

Vikki watched Fiona. It seemed like she wanted to say something. She inhaled, opened her mouth, then closed it again.

The bell rang.

Fiona got to her feet and went to open it. An older woman stood there, tears pouring down her face.

"I just heard. So sad, so sad," said the woman and hugged Fiona.

Gomez tapped Vikki's foot with hers. She nodded. It was time to go.

Vikki stood. Her eyes darted from Mr. Arden to Mrs. Arden. "Again, we're so sorry for your loss. We'll do our best to find out who did this and bring them to justice. If you remember anything that could help, please call us." Vikki handed Mrs. Arden her business card.

She took it and thanked her.

Gomez walked toward the door, and Vikki followed.

Vikki turned to Fiona. "Can I talk to you for a moment?" She continued for the door.

Fiona spoke to the woman who had just arrived. "Welcome, Aunt May. I'll be right back."

CHAPTER EIGHT

Fiona followed Vikki outside. The weather was overcast again. Vikki hoped it wouldn't rain and force the meeting that hadn't started to end.

Gomez brought out his cell phone. "I need to make a call. I'll be by the car." He walked away.

Vikki smiled. Gomez was a veteran, after all. She hoped she'd made the right call. That Fiona would open up to her. She smiled at Fiona as she approached. She and Paige had the same eyes and hair color, but that was where the resemblance ended.

Paige was tall—you could tell from her pictures, with symmetrical facial features. In contrast, Fiona was shorter, not yet thirty, and appeared ten years older.

Fiona must have felt like the older sister overshadowed by her beautiful younger sibling. Not everyone handled something they couldn't do anything about that well.

"Hi," Fiona said.

"I'm sorry about Paige. I wish there was something we could've done to prevent it." Vikki's tone was pleading. She took a deep breath and exhaled. "Was there something you held back because your parents were there?"

Fiona wrapped her light blue sweater tighter over her sunflower-print sundress. She took a deep breath and let it out in a sigh. "As our mother said, Paige didn't always believe she was pretty. She felt too tall that nobody liked her. When we were little, I was the outgoing one, but I didn't have her looks and charm. She had a way of making people laugh, drawing them out of their shells. Then came the first beauty pageant she won."

"While a senior in high school?" Vikki said.

Fiona nodded. "Everyone treated her differently after that. They wanted to be her friend. She got attention from people she knew and didn't know. Some offered her things—others wanted to take from her. At first, she didn't want any of that. But the genie was out of the bottle. Eventually, she embraced it, then couldn't get enough. At Rutgers, Paige became a party girl."

Vikki imagined a long-time caged dog suddenly unleashed. Unchecked, it would run free and wild.

Fiona paused—swallowed. "Paige is smart." A tear rolled down her cheek. "I can't believe she's dead."

Vikki didn't know what to say. "You mean, she wasn't who your parents thought she was? Like she was one person to them and another to her friends?"

Fiona nodded. "She was naive—too trusting. In college, she studied hard and played harder—a different picture from what people thought. She lived for Fridays and weekends. She flew to exotic places at the buzz of a text or ding of an email. London, Dubai, Paris, Monaco, Moscow, Hong Kong—you name it, she'd partied there."

Vikki kept her game face on. It sounded like she was describing somebody else.

"She hung out with the likes of famous people you see on

TV, *Vogue*, or *People Magazine*. I saw her passport once and thought it was a gag passport, full of stamps."

Vikki felt Fiona was in awe and probably jealous of her younger sister. Could she have murdered her? Jealousy was a powerful motive. Had Paige got caught up in the limelight? Engaged in unsavory activities to maintain a lifestyle she couldn't afford? The same type of situation a former contestant in *American Idol* had found herself in? Or used as a pawn by drug traffickers, and something had gone wrong?

She made a mental note to pull Paige's financial records and any records they could access. And see if any significant amounts of money had been exchanged.

"Where were you between seven and nine p.m. on Sunday?"

Fiona's nose flared. Her lips quivered, and she sobbed. Shoulder-shaking, deep, racking sobs. "I killed her."

CHAPTER NINE

Vikki stared for a few seconds, her mind devoid of thought. What was going on? She'd entertained the idea of Fiona being a suspect, but her confession was shocking. Vikki found her voice.

"Do you know what happened to your sister?"

"I killed her. I killed her," Fiona said amid sobs.

Vikki's heart pounded like a battering ram on a locked door. She glanced at Gomez. His back was to her. His phone pressed against his ear. Instinct took over. Her finger grazed the butt of her Glock. "What exactly are you saying?"

Fiona was shaking. "I was told to check on her when she didn't answer Mommy's call on Sunday night. I didn't go. I thought she'd spent the evening doing what she wanted to do. If only I had gone, maybe I would have saved her. Now she's dead." Fiona wailed. "If only I were there."

Vikki let out a shuddering breath. She placed her hands on Fiona's shoulders and tried to comfort her. *Don't think like that. You never know how things could have turned out. Instead of one daughter, your parents would be mourning two.* But Vikki didn't say that. Instead, she said, "Don't blame yourself. The blame is on the person who took her life. He's a coward."

"Coward?" Fiona said.

Vikki knew she'd said too much. But she couldn't stop now. "Paige had no defensive wounds." Her voice was quiet. "She was taken by surprise. Life always defends itself no matter what unless they don't see it coming."

"Oh God. Can I see her?"

Vikki remembered her friend, Alexis. She had been a sister to her. Vikki had been ten when Alexis's family had taken her in. She'd lost her mother and stepfather in a fire before then.

She had been bound for the foster care system when she'd met Alexis at the hospital where her father worked. They'd become fast friends, and Alexis wouldn't leave the hospital without Vikki.

Alexis had been strangled. Then Levin had said, "It's better you remember her the way you saw her, beautiful and kind." But Vikki had said no. She'd wanted to see. And they'd let her. What she saw made her want revenge.

Fiona's words pulled her out of her reverie.

"Can I?"

"We still need to make a formal identification on Paige. I'll talk to the medical examiner and make arrangements on when you can see her."

Fiona nodded and wiped her eyes with the back of her hand. "Sorry for the outburst."

"There's nothing to be sorry about. It's a tragedy." Vikki exhaled. "Is there anyone you think could have done this?"

Fiona exhaled. "She and Jessica are always going back and forth. They—"

The hairs on the back of Vikki's neck shot up. "Jessica Mills?"

Fiona's eyes widened. "Yeah." Her voice was high-pitched.

"They've been friends on and off since we were little. One minute you'll think they'll murder each other. The next, they're best of friends."

Vikki relaxed. "It was she who called nine-one-one. She was worried Paige hadn't come to school."

"Makes sense." Fiona shook her head. "Poor Jess. They were that tight. Then there's Greg Norris, who lives in the same apartment complex. She mentioned once that they entered the elevator at the same time, and he invited himself into her apartment. She said he was too forward. Tried to force himself on her."

Vikki brought out her notepad and scribbled on it. "Do you know if she filed a complaint?"

"I don't think so. She said he left after she threatened to call the police. But he gave her the creeps."

"Okay, we'll check him out. What about her boyfriend? Did she ever complain about him?"

Fiona thought for a moment. "She likes him a lot. Even if there were a problem, she'd endure it."

Vikki closed her notebook. "Thanks so much. Go back to your parents. You need each other. I'll do everything I can to ensure that whoever did this is brought to justice."

"What was that all about?" Gomez said when Vikki entered the car. "I saw your body language. Were you going to shoot her?"

Vikki started the Explorer and headed toward the road. "No, she blamed herself for her sister's death. Her mother had asked her to check on Paige when she didn't return her call last night. But she blew it off."

"Well, good thing she did. Their parents could be mourning two daughters now...or maybe none."

Vikki shot him a look. "None? Explain."

"The guy came, saw she had company and left. Who knows?"

Vikki headed back to the police station. "She mentioned a neighbor, Greg Norris. She said Paige alluded he once harassed her. They met on the elevator, and he invited himself to her house. He became too forward with her, and she asked him to leave."

"That wasn't the last she heard from him," Gomez said. "So he leaves, but he thinks: this is the one that got away. He returns to finish the job, but things get out of hand, and he kills her." Gomez inhaled and let out a sigh. "Yeah, let's surprise him first thing in the morning."

CHAPTER TEN

Vikki and Gomez got back to the station by six p.m. A different set of detectives were there. For Vikki, it was like she'd shown up to work but had never got to her desk. Thinking of it, the only thing she'd eaten was breakfast. She was hungry.

Gomez didn't bother going back into the office. He'd strolled over to his car to leave. Vikki reminded him of his umbrella.

"It can spend the night at the station. Tomorrow is another day. I need to eat, shower, and sleep. A dead dick cannot investigate anything. See you tomorrow, Mattsen, and get some sleep. I think tomorrow will be a busy day."

Vikki had agreed to a seven p.m. dinner date with Brandon. She went into the building and used the bathroom. She got in her car and headed home. It was six-thirty already. She could not get home, shower, change, and make it to the restaurant for seven.

Vikki remembered the text-to-speech feature on her phone. She took out her phone, tapped into the text field, and said, "Sorry, running late. See you at seven-thirty p.m." She hit send.

Unconsciously, she stepped on the gas. Her Explorer lunged forward. Going on a platonic date was uncharted territory for her. She rolled the engagement ring pendant on her necklace between her fingers. Was she doing the right thing? Was she opening her heart to something she'd vowed never to do again?

Granted, Dr. Brandon wouldn't be in the line of fire like Bruce had been, but anything could happen. She remembered what Gomez said his wife told him about her and Dr. Brandon. 'He likes her, and she likes him—what's the problem?'

Angie Baxter used Halley's Comet analogy to convince her to make a move. "If he moves on, by the time he comes back in seventy-four years, things would have changed completely."

Vikki pulled into the parking lot of the apartment complex she lived in. She took the elevator to the second floor and opened the door to her apartment at 204. She lived alone in a three-bedroom, two-and-half-bath apartment.

She locked the door behind her. Unconsciously, she took out her Glock and quickly swept the apartment. "Clear," she muttered when she was done. Was she paranoid, or did the idea of going on a date unnerve her?

Vikki went to the bathroom and turned the shower on. She put her Glock in the fingerprint biometric safe on her nightstand under her bed. She wouldn't forgive herself if an intruder broke in and shot her with her gun.

She was in and out of the shower and was dressing for dinner in a t-shirt and jeans when the doorbell rang.

Vikki froze.

It was like someone was playing a joke on her. Paige Arden's apartment came into focus. She retrieved her gun from the safe and tucked it behind her back.

She approached the door—cautiously.

Vikki peeped through the spy hole and did a double take. *"What the?"*

Now her pulse was a dog playing fetch, taking off at full speed after its favorite ball. She was in high school again, and this was her first date with her crush. She straightened out her hair, took a deep breath, and opened the door.

"Ted, what are you doing here?" She'd said Ted instead of Dr. Brandon.

"I got your text and thought, why not bring the food to you." He raised his hand, laden with a stapled brown paper bag.

Vikki opened her door wider. "Come in."

He walked past her. He smelled fresh and clean. Plus, a touch of cologne. The aroma of Chinese food followed. Her stomach rumbled as loud as a car driven on a flat tire.

"Wow, Vikki! That was resounding approval. I was worried you wouldn't be hungry."

"Get in here!"

Within minutes, they sat on her leather couch, the food spread out on the coffee table in her living room.

"I hope you like them. These are my favorites," Ted said.

He'd ordered some of her favorites too. Spring rolls, General Tso's chicken, shrimp with broccoli, sweet-and-sour pork, and chicken teriyaki. Brown rice, white rice, and egg fried rice.

Vikki dug in. "Mmh, the spring rolls are so crispy and tasty. You brought enough food to feed an army."

"You are an army of one." Ted shoveled food into his mouth.

Vikki gestured with her chopstick. "How was your day?"

"You just broke the rules," Ted said, smiling. "We said no talk about work."

"No, we agreed not to discuss cases." She got up. "Some wine?"

"Sure. Okay, work was busy. As you already know, I have a patient, a model. This is a nice segue into a topic I'm fascinated by. I've been meaning to ask you about your days on the runway, Runway. How did that happen?"

Vikki covered her face with the wine bottle and glass, feigning embarrassment. "Nobody at SIPD can keep a secret." She poured wine. "Tell me when."

Ted raised his hand when it was half full. She gave him the glass and poured one for herself.

"To new beginnings," Vikki said and raised her glass.

Ted said, "To new beginnings."

Their glasses clicked.

Vikki drank deeply, then put the wine glass down. "When I was in college, I spent two years on the Paris campus of my school. A guy I was dating then made me part of his work. Took pictures of me for his portfolio. Some decision-maker saw it in his portfolio and invited me to audition."

"Did you like it?"

"The glamour and attention were great," Vikki said. "But it's a cutthroat business. Constant competition among the girls. Hairspray, cigarette, drugs, men, women, ah— Runway."

Time flew as Vikki talked of that experience.

"That was awesome. You got the looks." He'd sung the words.

Vikki cocked her head. "Good imitation of Rick James. What about you? Med school, forensic pathology, private investigator, that's a book right there."

Ted got up. "We have to save something for a second date." He packed up the leftovers.

Vikki protested. "But this is not yet over."

"There's work tomorrow." He looked at the food. "There's still a lot left. We don't want to turn your fridge into a SIPD break room fridge. Take what you'll eat for tomorrow and next. I'll grab the rest."

A few minutes later, Ted was gone. She'd wanted to invite him back, to take advantage of her. But she knew he wouldn't make a move because he respected her.

Vikki didn't know when she fell asleep for the first time in a long time.

CHAPTER ELEVEN

The following day, Vikki had a spring in her step when she passed Jody's desk at the police station.

"Hi, Vikki. I don't think you're that happy to see me. Had a good evening?"

Vikki smiled. "I slept well."

"Good for you."

Santiago was leaving the detective squad room as Vikki entered.

Smiling, Santiago said, "I want whatever you had this morning."

Vikki headed for her desk. Her smile and her happiness faded when she got there. Someone had drawn a coffin on a piece of paper and left it on her desk. Written in the bold text were two words, *My condolences*. Vikki caught movement from the corner of her eye. It was McClane waving at her.

"I heard you lost a member of your Bimbo tribe. A runway model?"

Vikki glared at him. Heat flushed through her body. She took a step in his direction. "Paige Arden earned a BSc in mathematics from Rutgers! Until her death, she taught high school mathematics." Vikki shook her head. "You can make fun of me all you like, but why are you intimidated by a dead woman? Is it to get back to me? You are immature and disrespectful."

This time, the usual detectives who giggled when he made fun of Vikki did not. McClane had taken it too far. Even he knew that. Red-faced, he left the detective squad room.

Gomez walked in. "Hi." He pointed over his shoulder. "I saw McClane in the corridor. His face looked like a squeezed washcloth. What happened?"

Before Vikki could answer, the phone on her desk rang.

She picked it up. "Mattsen."

"Vikki?" There was a pause. "Is everything all right?" It was Levin.

Vikki inhaled and exhaled. "Yes, sir."

"Okay, I'll take your word for it. I need an update on the schoolteacher's murder. The church, the high school, the mayor, and the town council, are breathing down my neck. Bring Gomez with you to my office. At this rate, he's never going to retire." He hung up.

Vikki replaced the receiver and turned to Gomez. "He was disparaging a dead woman." She raised the drawing of a coffin. She knew she should save it as evidence if she decided to report him, but she shredded it to pieces. "I gave him a piece of my mind."

"Good for you." Gomez put down a tray with two cups of coffee and a paper bag.

Vikki smiled. "Thanks. The captain wants to see us."

Captain Neil Levin sat behind his executive desk, dressed in a navy-blue suit, as always, with a white shirt and red tie. "Do you have any suspects in custody?"

"Not yet, sir," Vikki said.

"We're gathering information and have a few leads to follow today," Gomez said.

Captain Levin raised a finger. "The spouse, one. Who else?"

"She's not married but in a relationship with Dr. Kevin Murdoch. He's an ER physician at Milton Medical Center. I called the hospital. He left for Los Angeles yesterday morning for a medical conference."

"Very convenient," Captain Levin said.

Vikki raised two fingers. "Her neighbor is number two. He lives in the same complex as the victim. The vic's sister said he and the vic had a run-in. We'll learn more about that soon. We sent a uniform to pick him up."

"We might look at the friend who discovered the body again," Gomez said. He looked at Vikki. "The victim's sister mentioned Paige was a party girl in college."

"Yes, but her friend, Jessica, didn't mention it, even though she was in school with her then."

"Maybe she's protecting her friend's reputation," Gomez said. "Only the living can protect the dead."

Vikki shook her head. "Not when we have a killer still out there."

Captain Levin pursed his lips. "I heard the scene was gruesome. Crime of passion?"

"It could be," Gomez said.

There was a knock on the door.

The captain raised an eyebrow. "Yes."

Detective Santiago stuck her head in. "Sorry to interrupt, sir. It's for Detectives Mattsen and Gomez. Greg Norris is in interview room one. A uniform just brought him in."

"Thank you, Maria," Gomez said.

She shut the door.

"All right, keep me updated."

Vikki got up. "Let's see what Mr. Norris has to say."

CHAPTER TWELVE

"He was about to enter his apartment when we got off the elevator," said Detective Santiago. "He saw us and took off like a rocket. Luckily, Detective John Wan was waiting downstairs for a move like that."

Vikki's eyebrows shot up. "John is back from vacation?"

"Yes. He tackled Mr. Norris. We then convinced him to come to the station to answer a few questions."

Vikki grinned. "Thanks, Maria." She walked over to the one-way window. She almost always checked out her opposition before going in.

Greg Norris was Caucasian, probably in his mid-twenties, about six feet two of all muscle, with green eyes and a thick beard. His sleeveless t-shirt was two sizes too small, completing his modern-day Viking persona. His tattooed arms crossed over his chest. He looked predatory and violent. Paige Arden had stood no chance with him.

Norris pursed his lips and transformed into a cuddly Koala. Vikki saw what had probably attracted Paige at first. Then he frowned and changed yet again. Had this mountain of a man walked in on Paige on Sunday night and murdered her to satisfy his lust?

They'd pulled his sheet. It showed four arrests and one conviction. Three were drug-related, and one was for assault.

Vikki, followed by Gomez, strolled into the interview room. Her eyes went to the ceiling to make sure the camera was on.

"I'm Detective Gomez, my partner, Detective Mattsen," Gomez said and sat to Greg Norris's left.

Vikki sat opposite him.

"Mr. Norris, why did you run from the police?" Gomez asked.

"Are you kidding me? It's eight a.m., and two people I know who don't live in the complex are zeroing in on me. My body told me what to do. Fight or flight? Two against one. If you add Mr. Jackie Chan I met downstairs, that's three. My odds were not good. I flew."

Vikki nodded. Mr. Norris sounded confident. His words were delivered matter-of-factly. She leafed through his folder, then glanced up. "Mr. Norris, what can you tell us about Paige Arden?"

"She's a tall hot beauty, and I'd love to know what her vault feels like."

"Okay, good," Gomez said. "We have your files here, and we know that Mary Forget once called the cops on you. You're no choir boy. Previous history of aggravated assault. What do you have to say to that?"

Greg shrugged. "Nothing. That was total nonsense. You didn't get to the part of the record where it said the charges were dropped. How do you kidnap and rape your girlfriend?"

"It's happened before," said Gomez.

"Not by me," Mr. Norris said. "We lived together. The relationship had gotten stale and wasn't working out. I told her I was moving on. Then she pulled the rape-and-kidnapping stunt on me. Of course, you guys quickly jumped to conclusions and grabbed my ass. She later dropped the charges, and we reconciled. I'd learned my lesson. The next time I made a move, I didn't say a word. I packed up my shit when she wasn't home. At dinner time, I ordered pizza and told her I would pick it up. That was six months ago. I'm sure she's still waiting for her Hawaiian Delight."

Gomez nodded. "What about Paige Arden?"

Greg Norris threw out his hands. "I told you already. Like the guys in the State Farm commercial, I'm a good neighbor. I wanted to know her better. She shot me down, and that was it."

The conversation went on for a good forty-five minutes without Greg alluding to any recent contact with Paige. Either he didn't know anything, or he was the world's best actor. Vikki was about to stop skirting around the issue and ask him flat out if he killed Paige, but Gomez was one step ahead and brought it up first.

Gomez exhaled and said, "I think I know what happened at her apartment, Greg. Sunday evening, either she invited you, or you invited yourself in. You were intent on feeling what her...getting to know her better, right? You wanted her —she wanted you. Then she changed her mind and said no. But you were too far gone. One thing led to another. Before you knew it, she was on the floor, not breathing."

Greg made a face like he'd just bitten into something sour. "What are you talking about?"

CHAPTER THIRTEEN

"You want to know what this is all about?" Vikki said. "It's about Paige Arden—and you showing up at her apartment."

Greg leaned forward. "Wait, did something happen to her? And she said I did it?"

"Paige is dead!" Gomez said.

"A witness is ready to testify that Paige mentioned you came to her apartment and tried to force yourself on her," Vikki said.

Greg tilted his head to one side and smiled. "This is a joke, right?" The smile on his lips faded. "Because I have no idea what you're talking about. Whatever it is, I assure you, I had nothing to do with it."

"If you're innocent, help us," Vikki said. "Where were you between seven and nine p.m. on Sunday?"

"Where were you?" Greg shot back. "You think I remember what I had for breakfast two hours ago? I can tell you this. I wasn't in anyone's apartment attempting to rape them, nor kill them. You guys are crazy. Wait, did you say she's dead? Like *dead?*"

"Yes, somebody murdered her in her apartment Sunday

night," Gomez said. "And we think you had something to do with it."

Greg's face turned white. The reality of the situation sank in. He ran his fingers through his hair. "This is serious." He pointed a finger in the air. "I see what is going on here. You guys have no suspects and are desperate for someone to pin it on. I can tell you right now that you're barking up the wrong tree. From seven p.m. to midnight Sunday, I was at work."

"And where is that?" Gomez asked.

"Misfits, a club in Morristown. I work there as a bouncer. At least a hundred people can vouch for me."

Vikki brought out her notepad. "What's the name of the place again?" She wrote it down.

Then Greg started talking.

"I met her once in the elevator. We got talking. I knew she was Miss Beauty and Brains or something like that. I'd never had a beauty queen, so I went for it. She's beautiful. It was easy. I showered her with praise. She was flattered."

Vikki hung on to his every word. Greg was talking fast.

"She invited me to her place. I remember she was staring at my tatts. Maybe she got scared. Next, she asked me to leave, and I did."

"This was on Sunday," Gomez said.

"No!" Mr. Norris sprang to his feet. "About a month ago."

Vikki and Gomez got up too.

"Sit down, Greg!" Vikki said.

He took a deep breath. His chest puffed out like a beer keg, and then he sat.

Vikki nodded. That was close enough to what Fiona said had happened. "Do you know who could have done this?"

Greg started shaking his head, then stopped. "You should be looking at her boyfriend. Some guy who visits her dressed in scrubs. Maybe he works as a technician or nurse in the hospital. I hear them yelling at each other."

Vikki raised an eyebrow. She remembered what Fiona had said. Paige wouldn't allude to problems, if any, between her and Kevin.

"About what?" Gomez asked.

"Jesus, how would I know? I heard angry voices."

Vikki believed him. He came across as a guy who'd found himself in a big body and searched for roles he could fit in. "We'll need to collect a DNA sample from you."

Greg thought for a moment. "I have nothing to hide. I don't mind. But I watched a documentary about O.J. Simpson and the planting of evidence. I don't want to take any chances. I need a lawyer."

CHAPTER FOURTEEN

Vikki, together with Gomez, spent almost two hours with Greg Norris. He said he needed a lawyer but permitted a cheek swab to obtain his DNA. He'd been ruled out as a primary suspect, so it wasn't a waste of time. The information gleaned from him helped turn the focus to Paige's boyfriend.

Vikki's coffee had become room temperature by the time she got to it. She wolfed down the donut and tried to drink the coffee cold. She couldn't. She went to the break room for the microwave. Vikki ran into Captain Levin, who was on his way out.

"Mattsen, how's the investigation going?"

"So far, so good. Some potential suspects have been downgraded, and some upgraded." Vikki raised her coffee cup. "Came to warm up my coffee."

"We can spare John Wan if you need more hands on deck. He just returned from vacation and is raring to go. Nothing like a homicide to keep one focused."

"Thank you, sir, that will be very helpful."

Vikki returned to her desk with her warm coffee. She'd

offered to heat up Gomez's, but he'd demurred. His cup was already empty.

Gomez pulled away from his computer. "I made some calls. Misfit, the nightclub in Morristown, confirmed Greg was there all night on Sunday. They could back it up with CCTV footage. I gave them your email."

"Nice. He sounded arrogant but truthful."

Gomez continued. "I called Jessica's parents. I got her mother. Jessica was there on Sunday, according to the mother. I asked if any other person had seen her at the house. She said the pizza guy."

"Yeah, I thought as much. We'll leave it as is for now. What about Milton Medical Center?"

"I called them. The conference Dr. Murdoch went to was booked eight weeks in advance. If he'd planned that far ahead, that gives premeditated a whole new meaning."

"Premeditated on steroids," Vikki offered.

"He's already on his way back."

Vikki raised an eyebrow. "Really. I thought he'd be on his way out of the country by now."

"Maybe he has nothing to hide. Or it's part of his plan." Gomez looked at a piece of paper. "He should be landing at Newark Liberty in the next two hours. I still have a few more things to tidy up here."

Vikki sighed. "Same here. It would be nice to pick him up at the airport." An idea crossed her mind. "I ran across the captain in the break room. He said everybody was breathing down his neck, as always. He offered extra human resources. John Wan is back. We can send him and a uniform to provide a welcome committee for the doctor."

Gomez's eyes brightened. "We should do that. John is good."

Vikki sat at her computer and went to work. Paige Arden's credit card information showed purchases in New

York on Saturday—no usage since Sunday. Vikki was looking forward to sitting across the room from Kevin Murdoch and hearing his story.

She continued to access different databanks, searching for information on Paige Arden. So far, she hadn't been successful. Time flies when you're having fun, they say. Vikki was surprised when John Wan walked up to her, all smiles. The last time she'd seen him was when he'd helped her clear folders from her desk after her vacation.

"Detective Mattsen, how are you?" John said, beaming.

"I'm good. Thanks for asking. You appear well-rested."

"Hi, John," Gomez said. They shook hands. "Good to have you back. I heard you're already kicking ass. I appreciate your help this morning."

"Thanks, John," Vikki said.

"Anytime, happy to be back," John said. "We're back from the airport. I'm happy to inform you that the eagle has landed and is safely in interview one, ready for you." He raised his hands. "No more thanks. I'm just doing my job. If you need me again, I'll be at my desk."

Gomez waved and turned to Vikki. "I guess we head to the interview room."

CHAPTER FIFTEEN

Vikki entered the interview room to a familiar odor. Sweet, fruity-rosy smell. She'd smelled that recently. But where? It was one of those times when you know you know something but can't access it in your mind.

"Hi, I'm Detective Victoria Mattsen." Vikki pointed at Gomez. "Detective Mike Gomez."

"Kevin Murdoch, MD."

They did not offer to shake hands.

Vikki sat opposite him, while Gomez sat to his left. Dr. Murdoch appeared to be in his early thirties. He had brown hair, brown eyes, and a one day stubble on his square jaw. An all-American type of guy with a life that seemed perfect from the outside. He was dressed for success in a form-fitting gray suit, and a white button-down shirt without a tie.

"Dr. Murdoch, do you know why you're here?" Vikki asked.

Kevin Murdoch cocked his head. "Please call me Kevin." He blinked rapidly. "The spouse is always looked at when one half is murdered. In this case, the boyfriend."

Vikki pursed her lips and nodded. "I'm sorry for your loss.

We have a few routine questions for you. When was the last time you saw Paige Arden?"

"Saturday night."

Gomez rested his elbows on the table. "Saturday night? Where? What did you do? Did you have sex?"

Vikki thought that was too aggressive, too soon. But Gomez was the veteran. Maybe he'd observed some body language from Kevin that had prompted him.

"W-why do you want to know?" Kevin said in a stutter.

"Come on, Doc," Gomez said, leaning back. "You should know this. Those swimmers can survive up to five days in there. If the ME comes across DNA in the victim, and they happen to be yours... This way, we know the reason why. Otherwise, that puts you at the crime scene."

Kevin shut his eyes tight. His hands balled into fists. He swallowed. "Was she raped?"

"The ME is still investigating," Gomez said. "You tell us now, and we get it out of the way. You don't need to come back if the question comes up."

Kevin exhaled and opened his eyes. "I understand. I was at Paige's apartment. We watched some TV. Yes, we had sex. I didn't use a condom."

Vikki asked a question she knew the answer to already. She wanted to hear his response. "Why did you run?"

Dr. Murdoch inhaled and let it out in a rush. "I did not run. The conference was scheduled in advance. You can check with the hospital's admin coordinator. I came back as soon as I heard."

"As I said, these are routine questions." Vikki maintained eye contact with him. Sometimes you could tell when a person was lying by their tells. "Where were you Sunday night between seven and nine?"

Dr. Murdoch hesitated. He took a deep breath and gave a loud sigh.

Vikki glanced down at her notepad, waiting. She raised her head when the silence lingered. "Kevin? Dr. Murdoch?"

"I was with Jessica," Dr. Murdoch said, his voice small.

Vikki's body hummed like a struck tuning fork. She remembered Jessica had said she was at her parents' home. "Sorry, with Jessica Mills? Where?" Pulse racing, she flipped through the pages of her notebook.

"Yes, with Jessica Mills." Kevin sounded more confident. "In my car at her parents' driveway."

Vikki swallowed hard, her body suddenly feeling heavy. She'd thought this was in the bag.

"How long did you stay there?"

"Emm...I'm not sure, from seven to maybe nine."

Gomez leaned forward, rubbing his hands together. "Will Jessica confirm what you said?"

Kevin threw out his hands, palms up. "Yeah, that's the truth. We were talking." He reached for a piece of paper in front of Gomez. "I'll write the address for you." He glanced around. "Pen?"

Vikki gave him a pen. He tilted the paper at an angle and wrote the address. Dr. Murdoch was a lefty.

"You can confirm with her anytime." Dr. Murdoch pushed the paper to Gomez.

"Nice penmanship," Gomez said. "What did you guys talk about?"

Vikki stared at him. She'd tried to figure out what to make of this. She looked away, then back to him. "Just talking?"

"Yes."

He didn't sound convincing, but Vikki had no more questions. She turned to Gomez. "Do you have anything for him?"

He shook his head.

"Okay, then we are done here." Vikki gave Murdoch her card. "If you remember anything, please don't hesitate to call."

Vikki's cell phone rang. Dr. Brandon flashed on the screen. "It's the ME," she said to Gomez. She got up and stepped out of the interview room. "Mattsen."

"Hi, this is Dr. Brandon here."

Vikki's pulse picked up a notch on hearing his voice. This was precisely one of her fears—her emotions. They'd agreed to always be professional at work, and she wasn't going to break it. "Hi, how can I help you?"

"Do you have a minute? I have new information for you and Gomez on Sunday's homicide victim."

"Sure. We'll be there in ten minutes." Vikki reentered the interview room. "The ME has something to show us."

Gomez got up. "I hope you're not going back to the conference?"

Dr. Murdoch did a slow, disbelieving shake of the head. "No, it's not like going to Newton Medical Center or Tisch Hospital in Manhattan for a conference."

"Anyway, don't leave town without letting us know," Gomez said. He did a head nod toward the door.

Dr. Murdoch got up.

Gomez held the door open. "Detective John Wan will drop you off."

CHAPTER SIXTEEN

The weather was nice, so they cut across the courtyard to the ME's office.

Vikki led the way. She walked past the receptionist, gave a quick wave, and went down to the morgue, where she was sure Dr. Brandon was.

They donned protective gear and entered. Feeling cold in there was a constant. The smell of autopsy chemicals was another constant.

Dr. Brandon was typing on the computer keyboard when they entered. "Hello, Detectives. Thanks for coming."

"We just let our main person of interest go," Gomez said.

Dr. Brandon raised an eyebrow. "The boyfriend?" It was a rhetorical question. "You can pick him up again when you have evidence. Discovering the cause of an illness and crime have a lot in common. They both start with an investigation, and the process is evidence-driven."

"What do you have for us?" Vikki said.

Dr. Brandon walked over to the autopsy table with Paige Arden on display. Her body was cleaned. Her skin still had the marks made by the knife. In addition, she now sported the Y-shaped baseball thread scar.

"The victim died from her wounds, and they were numerous," Dr. Brandon said. "The attack was sudden. She never saw it coming. She has no defensive wounds."

Vikki's heart pounded as if she were experiencing violence right now. That was precisely what the CSU head had said, no defensive wounds.

"The perpetrator was very angry or was in a frenzy. She was stabbed fifty-four times. One lung was deflated. Her voice box was crushed. She had significant trauma to the head. Her skull was fractured in many places."

Gomez let out a loud sigh, shaking his head.

Dr. Brandon continued. "She would have bled to death if left alone. But she was strangled. The imprint from the sock was on her neck."

Vikki let out a strangled breath. "What about the rape kit?"

Dr. Brandon shook his head. "She was raped. But he'd used a condom. We recovered some identifying chemicals from her vagina. Nonoxynol-9, and—"

"Spermicide?" Gomez threw up his hands. "Every condom has it. The perp's lawyer would walk all over that if this ended up in trial."

Dr. Brandon nodded. "I know. But nonoxynol will be in conjunction with another lubricant we found called pulegone."

Vikki's eyes narrowed. Hope surged in her heart. Anything that could be leveraged to find the perp was welcome.

"It gives lubricants a raspberry smell. Find a suspect with that in his glove compartment or toilet bag, and that narrows it down further."

"Or turns a person of interest into a suspect," Vikki muttered.

"Thanks, Ted," Gomez said. "You've given us food for thought."

"Oh, I almost forgot. Based on the angle the knife was plunged into her back, the perp is likely left-handed."

CHAPTER SEVENTEEN

Vikki was on her way home. From the morgue, she'd returned to her desk to catch up on reports. It'd been a day with many activities that seemed to go nowhere. Before they left the morgue, she'd asked Dr. Brandon one question.

"How much of science is the theory about the perp being left-handed? You said based on the angulation of the knife?"

"It's more or less a guideline. Based on the laws of probability, a right-handed individual could produce a left-handed-like stab result depending on attempts. It's like tossing a die. You don't hit six on every throw. But you will as long as you keep on trying."

After that, Gomez said he was done for the day and left.

Vikki called Angie.

"Hello, Vikki, do you have news for me?" her voice blared from the car's speakers.

"No, I was wondering if you heard anything about the murder. You are the news hound dog."

There was a pause. "That better be a compliment. If I ever find out you referred to me as a dog... You should be the one checking yourself for fleas."

Vikki smiled. She'd walked straight into that one.

"Guess who I saw last night at the Chinese restaurant? With enough food to feed an army. And he wasn't going to Camp Lejeune or Picatinny Arsenal."

Now Vikki laughed. Oh God, as if she wasn't already having a messed-up day. Now she had to add Angie to it.

Something dashed across the road. Her headlamp showed the white tail of a doe. "Damn deer."

"What did you say?"

Vikki was about to heave a sigh of relief when another deer followed. It all happened within seconds.

This was a massive male with big antlers. Vikki's stomach all but slammed into her heart, and she hit the brakes. She'd forgotten her driving mantra. Never brake for any animal that runs onto the road. Easier said than done. Her Explorer swerved onto oncoming traffic, then back onto her lane. She'd narrowly missed a head-on collision with a yellow school bus.

Her whole body was shaking, and her breathing came in spurts. She slowed down.

"Vikki? Vikki? Are you there? I heard loud, sharp breathing. What happened?"

"A deer dashed into the road, pursued by another. I lost control and nearly ran into a school bus." Vikki exhaled.

"Wow, thank goodness you're okay. Those deer. Something has to be done."

"I thought peak mating season for deer in New Jersey ran from late October through November. And ends just before Christmas."

"Vikki, you said peak. Males are always trying to get some tail whenever they see it."

Vikki's gaze was glued to the side of the road. She wasn't taking chances. Talking of tail, should she tell Angie about the interview earlier at the police department?

Was Dr. Murdoch a buck? Allegedly getting it on with his

girlfriend's best friend forever (BFF)? A picture of tomorrow's *St. Ives Examiner* flashed in her mind—NJ DOCTOR IN MURDER LOVE TRIANGLE. No way.

"Vikki, are you there?"

"Yes, yes. A bit shaken by the close encounter of the deer kind. Let me call you back."

"Okay, drive safe."

Vikki hung up.

She took it slow and steady until she got home.

The smell of Chinese food from last night still lingered in the air. Gun in hand, she swept her apartment, room by room. Nobody was there. It felt like it'd been ages since she'd left. The events of last night came back to her. She'd done well at work when she'd gone to see Ted at the morgue. No public display of affection.

Vikki put her gun away and turned on the shower to warm up. She returned to the kitchen, poured some rice, chicken, and vegetable mix onto a plate, and popped it into the microwave.

She took a shower, got her food, and ate in the living room with the TV on. Vikki channel surfed, then settled on the local station. As if on cue, Paige Arden was on the news. They showed Captain Levin talking to a reporter.

"This is Captain Levin of St. Ives Police Department," the reporter said. "Captain, any leads on the brutal murder of the current Miss St. Ives Beauty and Brains, and math professor at St. Martins Academy?"

"Our hearts go out to the family of Paige Arden. We are following a few leads, which I cannot discuss because it's part of an ongoing investigation. But I'll keep you updated as we discover answers. We'll do our best to bring the person or people responsible for this senseless act to justice. Thank you."

St. Martins Academy, thought Vikki. They hadn't looked at it yet.

CHAPTER EIGHTEEN

Vikki left her apartment early. The plan was to lay a solid foundation food-wise before the day started. She wore her usual outfit, pantsuit, and her Glock. She stopped at Dunkin' and got two large coffees and two breakfast sandwiches. She hoped Salina wouldn't murder her for feeding Gomez.

"This is good," Gomez said.

They were in the detective squad room. They hadn't planned it, but they'd both arrived early.

Gomez chewed and swallowed. "Sausage, egg, and cheese on a croissant, my favorite. So, you're suggesting we pick up Jessica Mall and run what Dr. Kevin said through her? Also, get an interview with the principal of the school?"

Vikki had signed out a nondescript Ford Vogue from the police station's small fleet, and they drove to St. Martins Academy. Vikki found a spot in the parking lot. It was primarily filled with luxury cars. Vikki didn't think they belonged to the teachers. Their sheer number meant they belonged to the students—gifts from their wealthy parents.

The whole school was one massive fifties- and sixties-era style building. Different sections were added over the years, evident by the slight change in style and color of the bricks. It had a state-of-the-art football field, tennis court, and baseball field. She was positive a fantastic basketball court was located somewhere inside the building.

Vikki and Gomez strolled up the hedge-lined walkway to the main entrance. Since school shootings have become an epidemic in the US, visitors must be buzzed in, registered, and escorted to where they need to be.

Vikki hit the bell.

A uniformed guard appeared at the window. Bald, middle-aged with a Pancho Villa-style mustache. He looked at them with a welcoming smile.

Vikki raised her badge for the guard to see. A glass wall with a door separated the visitor from entering the school building.

There was a buzz and a click, and the door opened. They entered another section, the foyer. They talked to the guard, but still no access into the building—another glass wall with a door separating them. It reminded Vikki of visiting the correctional facility to see an inmate.

Vikki introduced them. "I'm Detective Mattsen—my partner, Detective Gomez. We're here on a homicide investigation."

"I'm Larry Eastland. It's such a sad affair what happened to our Queen—Ms. Paige. She was such a lovely girl—always said good morning to me in a sing-song voice when she came through this door."

He passed a clipboard to them with a sheet that said: *visitors log*. Vikki wrote her name, when she'd arrived, who she was coming to see, and the date and time. She signed her signature. Gomez did the same.

"Did you see her on Friday?" Gomez asked.

"Yes!" Mr. Eastland said. "Paige is royalty here. I remember her smiling face as if she's on the runway."

Gomez nodded. "Any signs of jealousy with other faculty? Or students who are infatuated with her because of the pageant and want to get closer? Or those who are upset that they got bad grades in math? Not everyone is good at math."

"I hear you. Our kids are good. The teachers are cordial with one another. If there are any animosities, they're not publicly expressed."

"I do have some routine questions for you," Vikki said. "It's part of the process."

Mr. Eastman closed his eyes and nodded. "I understand. Are you the detective who investigated the murder at the circus several months ago?"

Vikki raised an eyebrow. "Yes, why?"

"My buddy, Jon Jackson. We work for the same security agency. He discovered the victim. He speaks highly of you."

The slight twitch on Vikki's lips grew into a smile. "Thank you."

"What about me?" Gomez said. "I was part of the team. He didn't mention me?"

The security guard smiled. "I'll ask him when I see him again."

"I'm taking over the questioning," Gomez said.

"Ask away!"

"Where were you on Sunday between seven and nine p.m.?"

"I was home with the kids and wife roasting marshmallows in the backyard." He pulled out his phone and showed Gomez time-stamped photos and video of him over a fire with a boy and girl on each side holding marshmallows on sticks over a fire. He texted them to Gomez.

"I wish I could help," Mr. Eastman said. "We've lost our royalty. I can't stop thinking about her."

Gomez gave him his card. "You can call me for whatever reason."

"Thank you." Mr. Eastman let out a breath. "Since I've confirmed you're bona fide, Ms. Turner's office is down the corridor to your right. You can't miss it. It has a big sign on the door that says Vice Principal."

"It's a pleasure meeting you," Vikki said. "My regards to your colleague when you see him."

She headed down the corridor, shoulder to shoulder with Gomez. Their heels made *click-click* sounds on the terrazzo floor.

"Someone's attained celebrity status."

"I don't know about that. I know that on Friday, Paige Arden walked down these hallowed halls and left the building —never to return. And the person or persons responsible is still roaming free."

CHAPTER NINETEEN

Vikki looked ahead. The door the security guard had mentioned was as described. The St. Martins Academy corridor smelled of disinfectant, polish, and something flowery.

She and Gomez passed a few students—the girls in polo shirts and short plaid skorts. The boys looked formal in button-down shirts and ties and dark brown pants.

Vikki knocked on the slightly open door.

"Come in," said a female voice.

A tall African American woman in business attire, pantsuit, her hair in braids, smiled at them. She was probably about Vikki's age, thirty-two.

"Hello, I'm Jane Turner, the assistant vice principal. Welcome to St. Martins Academy." She walked around the desk, hands extended.

"I'm Detective Mattsen, and my partner, Detective Mike Gomez."

They shook hands.

Ms. Turner pointed them to the two chairs opposite the table and returned to hers.

"Sorry, the principal had a last-minute meeting and asked me to meet with you. I hope I'll be able to help. It's so sad and tragic what happened to Paige."

"What can you tell us about Ms. Arden?" Vikki said. She sat on one of the chairs.

"Paige is well-liked. I was here when she joined the faculty straight out of college. She has the heart of a teacher and loves teaching. People she grew up with said she used to be shy. I think the pageant thing is more like a hobby."

Gomez made a steeple with his hands. "Did she get along with other teachers? Any anger, resentment?"

"Not at all," Ms. Turner said. "Most people, including me, are in awe of her. She could have gone anywhere to teach or go into another field. But she chose to give back. It's not every time an alumnus comes back to teach. Most feel stifled by the town, especially if they grew up there, too."

Vikki nodded. "That makes sense."

"I would also," Ms. Turner said. "But I'm not a beauty queen and not getting all the attention that comes with it. You know, the big fish in a small pond."

That was an angle Vikki had never thought of. She leaned forward. "That's what's baffling. Why would someone want to end her life if she brings a lot of positivity?"

Ms. Turner threw out her hands, shaking her head. "The academy's strength in sports and academic performance is a major draw for new students. But Paige Arden and her friend, Jessica Mills, are our claim to social media fame."

"How's that?" Gomez asked.

"Paige won Ms. Beauty and Brains, while Jessica was runner-up. Two beauty queens, and they are teachers from the same institution? It is a big boost to us."

That was news to Vikki. She never knew Jessica contested, too.

"We have some routine questions to ask," Gomez said.

Ms. Turner's eyes focused on his, waiting.

"Did Ms. Arden have any recent problems with students or faculty? Has she received threats in any form from students or faculty? Any signs of addiction, stress, or abnormal behavior? Has she shown favoritism to any student?"

As Gomez rattled off his questions, Ms. Turner's lips were pursed, her head shaking from side to side.

"That's a no to all?"

"Detective Mattsen, Paige was well-liked. She was one of those people who loved to please others. Get them talking about themselves and their plans. And genuinely interested in what they have to say.

"She boosted the interest of our boys in math after she won Miss Brains and Beauty. We've seen a few pics of her competing in a swimsuit taped to boys' lockers." She gave a helpless shrug. "What can I say? Boys will be boys."

"It seems like there was civility among the boys," Gomez said. "We were never called for disorderly conduct."

Vikki's thoughts centered on what-ifs.

Ms. Turner continued. "We were a bit worried, this being a religiously affiliated school. But we put it in prayer and hoped it came to pass. Then this..." She covered her mouth with both of her hands.

Vikki let out a deep breath. The three of them reached the same conclusion at the same time. Any of the male students could have followed her home—claimed they had a math problem, and she buzzed them in.

Had Vikki unwittingly opened a can of worms? It would be a nightmare to interview all her students. The pushback from parents. The uproar it would trigger. She didn't want to think about it. There must be another way.

Vikki and Gomez decided to make the best of their time there. They started with faculty. By the end of their appointment at the school, they'd talked to half a dozen teachers and gotten zero new leads. They called it a day.

The need to interview up to a hundred students was beginning to look like a bad dream come true. They headed for the exit.

Jessica Mills was walking in front of them, her hair in a ponytail. Vikki hadn't known she was in school. Getting her to throw more light on Dr. Murdoch's whereabouts on Sunday evening might hold the key to solving this murder.

"Excuse me. Jessica!"

CHAPTER TWENTY

"We didn't know you were here," Vikki said. "We were about to visit you at home."

Jessica exhaled. "I thought I'd come in and work. Keep my mind busy and forget the image I saw. But that didn't work. Easier said than done. It was all I was thinking of."

They agreed to drive to the police station instead. By four-forty p.m., Vikki had Jessica Mills in interview two. She got a bottle of water and Coke from the vending machine. She must be watching what she put in her body. She offered her both drinks. Jessica accepted the Coke.

"Thank you," Jessica said. She unscrewed the bottle and drank deeply. When she lowered the bottle, the Coke was halfway gone. "Wow. I didn't know I was that thirsty." She screwed the cap back on. "How long did you say this is going to take?"

"Probably a few minutes at the most," Vikki said. It wasn't a lie or the truth. They would keep her until they got answers. She'd asked Gomez to observe from the observatory deck.

Vikki started with the big surprise of the day. "I didn't know you were into pageantry, too."

"It's more of a hobby for me." Jessica smiled. "I did it mainly to support Paige. She's the pretty one. But she never knew it. In high school, our friends urged Paige to enter a beauty competition. Paige wouldn't do it. 'I'm an ugly duckling.'" Jessica mimicked Paige's voice. "To support her, we all joined. The ugly ducking turned into a swan." A tear rolled down Jessica's cheek. She sniffed and wiped her eyes with the back of her hand.

Vikki smiled. "So, that's how you got into modeling, too."

Jessica nodded. She talked some more about her and Paige. Vikki didn't interrupt. It reminded her of her and Alexis. They had a lot in common, and the friendships ended prematurely in death.

When she felt she'd gained enough rapport with Jessica, she threw in the stick of dynamite. Vikki believed talking to the students at St. Martins was inevitable, but she'd try.

Vikki focused on Jessica. Ready for any body language that might indicate she was lying. "We interviewed Dr. Murdoch, Kevin."

Jessica nodded.

"He said he came to see you at your parents' house. Is that true?"

Jessica hesitated. She took a sip of Coke. "Yes, he came from the hospital. He was upset. He said he'd lost a patient."

Vikki exhaled. "What time was that?"

"The pizza delivery guy had come and gone before he came. He said he had to leave early the next day for a conference in Los Angeles. And he hadn't prepared his talk." Jessica pursed her lips. "Probably around nine p.m."

Vikki's inside tightened. Adrenaline shot through her. She steadied her voice. "He came around nine?" Her eyes darted to the one-way window and back to Jessica.

"Yes." Jessica's eyebrows narrowed. She followed Vikki's

gaze to the window and back to Vikki. Her ponytail bounced from one shoulder to the other. "W-what did I say?"

Vikki was on her feet. "I'll be right back, Jessica. Sit tight. Do you need another Coke?"

She shook her head. Her lips and chin quivered. She looked like a marshmallow stabbed with a skewer, about to be roasted over an open flame.

CHAPTER TWENTY-ONE

Vikki checked the time on her phone one more. It was six-fifteen p.m.

She and Gomez rushed to Milton Medical Center for an audience with Dr. Kevin Murdoch. He'd been upgraded from a person of interest to the main suspect. No matter how things panned out tonight, the least he'd be charged with was obstruction.

Dr. Murdoch was in the OR when Vikki and Gomez arrived. They waited for him to finish. He'd changed and was down to baby-blue scrubs and clogs when he stepped out of the changing room. Vikki began the persuasion process.

"Dr. Murdoch, we have some questions for you at the police station," Vikki said.

"It's up to you, Kevin," Gomez said. "We can cuff you in front of your patients and colleagues, or you can come peacefully, and this misunderstanding will be straightened out at the station."

Dr. Murdoch chose the latter.

Vikki was surprised he didn't ask questions or scream for

a lawyer. Personally, if she were ever arrested, she'd ask for a lawyer pronto.

Vikki, Gomez, and Dr. Murdoch got to the PD safely. But when they stepped into the corridor on their way to interview him, Miss Mills was there, too. Her eyes almost popped out of their sockets.

"Kevin? Kevin...did you lie to me? What did you do?" Jessica said, her voice shaky. Her whole body trembled.

Dr. Murdoch's eyebrows narrowed. "What are you doing here? What's this all about?"

"We'll get to the bottom of it soon," Gomez said. He turned to the good doctor. "At what time did you get to Jessica Mill's parent's home on Sunday?"

Kevin glared at Jessica. "What did you tell them?"

Jessica's hand flew to her mouth. "Kevin, what did you do?"

"I'll tell you," Vikki said. She said you got to her parent's home around nine p.m. Paige was murdered between seven and nine p.m. You just had enough time to do it. You went home, showered and changed, then rushed to her as your alibi."

Dr. Murdoch lunged at Jessica. "That's not true! She's lying. I didn't go there!"

Gomez grabbed him.

Jessica's face turned green. "Oh my God, oh my God... Paige...Kevin, you didn't." Her voice cracked as she spoke. "I'm going to be sick."

"You didn't go there, right?" Gomez said. "Why don't you come in and tell us your side of the story?" He led him into interview one.

Vikki attended to Jessica.

"I'm all right," Jessica said moments later. "Did he do it?"

Vikki let out an exasperated sigh. "Listen to me. I don't know. This is an ongoing investigation. Nothing you heard here is concrete." She exhaled. That was one of the reasons why interviews were done in interview rooms. "I'll have Detective Wan take you home."

"I feel a lot better. I can drive myself."

Vikki watched her disappear through the exit. Then she headed for the interview room. Gomez was talking.

"Kevin, sometimes these things happen," Gomez said. "These things happen. She told you about a relationship that got you upset, you snapped, and before you knew it, she was dead."

"I told you, I wasn't there," said Dr. Murdoch.

There was a tap on the window.

"I'll take care of it." Vikki excused herself.

It was Mallory from the CSU. He handed Vikki a piece of paper.

Vikki read it. Her head jerked up.

Mallory had a big smile on his face.

Vikki's pulse picked up a notch. "My goodness. I can't believe it." She sounded breathless.

"That's the paper equivalent of a smoking gun," Mallory said.

Vikki reentered the interview room. "Dr. Kevin Murdoch, please stand up."

He stood slowly, forehead furrowed. "What's going on?"

Vikki walked over to him. "Interlock your hands behind your head."

"What?" Dr. Murdoch said. "Are you arresting me?" The words came out as a strangled cry.

Vikki removed her handcuffs. "Kevin Murdoch, you're under arrest for obstruction and the murder of Paige Arden. You have the right to remain silent. Anything you say can and will be used against you in a court of law. You have the right to an attorney." Vikki read him the rest of his rights as she cuffed him.

Gomez picked up the paper Mallory had brought in.

"I didn't do it," Dr. Murdoch said. "Jessica's trying to get back at me."

Gomez snorted. "Get back at you for what?"

"Because I dumped her for Paige."

"Now your memory has become very sharp," Gomez said. "But the evidence against you is damning. Your fingerprint was found on Paige's cowboy boots. A jury of your peers will be happy to put you in a cage."

Dr. Murdoch stood with a slightly stooped posture. His hands were behind his back. His shoulders slumped. "I was there, but I didn't kill her." His voice was a flat monotone.

CHAPTER TWENTY-TWO

Dr. Murdoch was intent on talking. As a precaution, Gomez Mirandized him a second time. Vikki's gaze drifted to the ceiling. The camera lights were on. It was recording.

"Statistics tells us that the spouse did it, but I didn't. Just that my alibi sucks," Dr. Murdoch said.

"Really. We have plenty of time," Vikki said. "Why don't you tell us what statistics got wrong."

Murdoch chuckled.

Vikki hoped he wouldn't backtrack and ask for a lawyer. "Tell us what happened."

Dr. Murdoch said, "I had a date with Paige. We'd planned to eat a late dinner and return to her apartment. When I arrived at her apartment, her door was open."

"How did you get into the building?" Vikki asked. She admonished herself for interrupting him. You don't interrupt a suspect talking freely—questions after.

"I pushed the button for three hundred and two every ten seconds. When she didn't buzz me in after the third time, I pushed all the buttons. Someone let me in. When I got upstairs, her door was slightly open. I thought she must be in the shower and left the door open for me."

Vikki wanted to know what time it was but didn't want to spook him.

"I checked the time on my phone," Dr. Brandon said. "It was after eight forty-five p.m. I smelled it right away. Blood and disinfectant. For a second, I thought I was back in the OR. The smell led to the bedroom—where I found her." Dr. Brandon's voice cracked. "I rushed over and kneeled beside her. A cowboy boot rested on her neck. I moved it to check her carotid. There was no pulse." His voice seemed to fade away. He stopped speaking.

Gomez prompted him. "What did you do?"

Dr. Brandon inhaled and exhaled. "I realized the situation I was in. It looked like I did it. All I had to do was pull out my phone and call nine-one-one."

Vikki nodded.

"But the image of Harrison Ford in *The Fugitive* was pinned on my mind. A physician was accused of killing his wife. I ran. Only when I got home did I notice there was blood on me. I took off my clothes. Put them in the fireplace and set them on fire."

Gomez cleared his throat. "You burned them?"

Dr. Murdoch nodded. "Then I took a shower and went to see Jessica."

"And she was expecting you with open arms," Vikki said.

Dr. Murdoch exhaled. "We used to date. I left her for Paige." He shrugged. "In retrospect, I should have just stayed at my home. That's it. I went home, and the following day I left for LA as planned. That's what happened."

Vikki pursed her lips. "You're not holding anything back?"

"No secrets?" Gomez said.

Dr. Murdoch shook his head.

"Anyway, it doesn't matter," Vikki said. "Once we get the warrant, by this time tomorrow, you won't have any secrets. Book him."

CHAPTER TWENTY-THREE

Dr. Murdoch was booked. His picture was taken. He swapped his baby-blue scrubs for jail clothing and was taken across the courtyard to the correctional facility where he'd spend the night.

By the time Vikki got into her dependable Ford Explorer and headed home, it was ten forty-five p.m. Her stomach growled, reminding her that the foundation she'd laid in the morning was gone. Eating Chinese food for the third consecutive night didn't appeal to her. A Burger King was coming up, and Vikki decided to go through the drive-thru.

Her phone rang. It was her Ted, Dr. Brandon. It was funny the way she thought about him. At work, he was the ME. At night he became her Ted.

"Hi, Ted. Hold on one second. I'm about to order some food."

"How can I help you?" a male voice came through the speakers.

"Two Whopper Jrs and a small Sprite, please."

The voice repeated what she'd ordered and said to pull up to the window.

"Why didn't you get a Whopper instead of two Jrs?" Ted asked.

"Whopper Jrs are so juicy. We'll discuss this again after you try it." She collected her food, took a sip of the drink, and sighed as the liquid cooled everything on its way down. "I'm so hungry. Talk to me. I apologize in advance for munching in your ear." As Vikki drove and ate, she kept an eye on the side of the road. She didn't want any more encounters with a horny deer.

"Busy day at work today?"

Vikki chewed and swallowed. "We have a suspect in custody."

"Wow! No kidding. That's good news."

"The boyfriend, Dr. Murdoch. He'd lied to us earlier about his alibi, then CSU investigators matched his fingerprints to a blood smear on her cowboy boot. He admitted he was there, but he didn't do it."

Dr. Brandon laughed. "The classic defense strategy—Some Other Dude Did It."

"SODDI," Vikki said. "Anyway, we'll search his apartment tomorrow as we build a case. He claimed he burned what he was wearing, but we'll see. Criminals always make mistakes." But, in her mind, she wasn't so sure. Doctors are healers, not killers.

"Okay, Vikki, I'm going to let you go to focus on your driving. Last night I almost ran into a deer. Have a good night."

He hung up before Vikki could respond. A few minutes later, her phone rang again. This time it was Angie. It was like she did her socializing in her car on her way back.

"Hi, Angie. You're still awake?"

"Of course. I'm a crime reporter. Crime never sleeps."

Vikki laughed. "I should know that. I'm on my way home. It was a long day." She told Angie a watered-down version of her trip to the St. Martins Academy and finding out Jessica Mills was into pageants, too. "We have a suspect in custody."

"What! That's what you should have told me first instead of stories about teenage boys and their hormones. Who?"

Vikki told her. "But please keep his name out of it for now. Just say a person of interest is in custody."

"Why?"

"I don't know. Deep in my gut, I think he might be telling the truth. It doesn't make sense."

"It doesn't need to make sense to you," Angie said. "It makes sense to the doer."

"Why do you stab your girlfriend fifty-four times, have sex with her, then strangle her?"

"She was stabbed that many times? Oh, my goodness. Mattsen, you've been holding out on me."

Vikki sighed. She'd better stop talking before she gave Angie her social security number, too.

"Anyway, I called because I have something for you. Earlier today, I heard from the grapevine that a model/beauty pageant queen was murdered in Beckham Township, New Jersey. Initially, I thought it was your case until they mentioned the town. Maybe it's a coincidence."

Vikki was alert. She'd learned from experience. Crime was rarely a coincidence. She turned into the parking lot of her apartment complex.

"Vikki, are you there?"

"Yes, yes. Sorry, I was thinking of what you said."

"Just food for thought. I share information and not hold out, unlike others I know."

Vikki sighed. "Come on, Angie. You know my hands are tied."

"That's fine. I'll dig more into this in case there's a bigger picture. Talk tomorrow."

Vikki's thoughts were jumbled up when she walked into

her apartment. Dr. Brandon, a similar case—sleep might not come easy. But once she showered, put on her pjs, and got in bed, she closed up like a tulip at night.

CHAPTER TWENTY-FOUR

Vikki sat opposite Captain Levin in his office by nine a.m. Thursday. She wore black cotton pants and a cream blouse. A gray sports blazer hid her holstered Glock clipped onto her belt.

"I need this investigation moving at the speed of sound," Captain Levin said. He was in his navy-colored suit as always. He paused for a moment. "Has he called a lawyer?"

Vikki shook her head.

"We'll have to appoint one for him, then."

There was a knock on the door. Gomez walked in.

Captain Levin held up a piece of paper. "If the good doctor is a bad influence on society, evidence is our best friend. The search warrant for his car and home is ready." He handed the pieces of paper to Vikki. "Do what you need to do and do it right. When he hires a lawyer, he will go for the best. We don't want to give them any 'gotcha' opportunities."

Gomez grinned. "Thank you, sir. We'll rip him a new asshole."

After two and a half hours, the inside of Dr. Murdoch's

three-bedroom home looked like a demolition crew had placed dynamite sticks in the wrong house.

Chief of CSU, Dennis Mallory, and three investigators working in the living room, dining room, and kitchen. Vikki, Gomez, and Detective John Wan tore the room apart. It didn't take long to create a huge mess. They pulled out sofas and drawers. Removed paintings from the walls—everything was searched.

The fireplace did have ashes and remnants of a recent fire. Mallory collected them all. There was no smoking gun.

"The man does love his Hostess Raspberry Zingers," One of the CSU investigators said. "There were packs of it everywhere."

"When I picked him up at the airport," Detective Wan said, "he had two packs as we drove to the PD. They were gone by the time we arrived."

Vikki felt like she'd been jerked awake while napping in a moving car that had stopped suddenly. Was that the cause of the raspberry smell? Did they have the wrong person? But his fingerprints were there.

Back at the police department, Mallory and his crew took what they'd collected back to the forensic department to sift through. Vikki returned to her desk while Gomez left the squad room, murmuring something about the break room.

Vikki got on her computer. What Angie had said last night was burning a hole in her head. Since Murdoch's home hadn't yielded any secrets, she should look at other possibilities. She searched on Google. And there it was—yesterday's *Beckham Township Examiner*. PRETTY DEAD: Reigning beauty queen of a local pageant in Beckham Township, New Jersey, was murdered.

. . .

Twenty-three-year-old Brie Dallas was discovered early this morning on Peach Road by a motorist on his newspaper route. He noticed the car parked at the side of the road with the driver's and passenger's doors open. He stopped to render assistance but found no one. The vehicle was in disarray, and blood was everywhere. He immediately called 911. The police suspect foul play. When they popped the trunk, they found the victim's naked body. According to her friends, Brie was well-liked and had completed a photo shoot to begin the next phase of her life in modeling. Please call the sheriff's HOTLINE number if you have any information that could help solve this crime.

Goosebumps erupted on Vikki's arm—after a photoshoot in New York. This couldn't be a coincidence. She reread the story, shaking her head. When she was done, she picked up her phone and dialed Angie.

"Baxter."

"Angie, this is Vikki—I just read about the girl murdered in Beckham. It's similar to what happened to Paige."

"I was going to call you," Angie said. "I did more research. It seems like someone is murdering beauty queens all over the country. Small towns within an hour's drive from a major city. Some went missing and were never found. Others were found murdered. We might have a serial killer on our hands."

Vikki blew out a breath. "Jesus, I'll call the Beckham police department to find out more. If the MOs are similar, we could have a serial killer on the loose. Let's talk later. Bye." Vikki hung up. It was too early to call the FBI. She didn't have answers to the questions they'd ask.

She Googled Beckham Township police. The sheriff's office came up. Yes, she almost forgot. They had a sheriff over there. She tapped the phone icon. It began to ring.

CHAPTER TWENTY-FIVE

Vikki called the sheriff's office at Beckham Township but got the secretary.

"Sheriff Alison Slater is not here right now, but if you can leave your name, number, and message, I'll make sure she gets it."

Vikki didn't know they'd changed sheriffs. The one she knew was Sam Gordon. She left a message for her to call as soon as possible and that she thought the murder of the young woman was connected to a murder here in St. Ives.

Gomez walked into the squad room as Vikki hung up. He flopped into his chair and faced her. "You look...harassed." He glanced around the squad room. "But I don't see McClane. Everything okay?"

In reply, Vikki turned her monitor screen to face him.

Gomez read fast. "You think they're related? It does have a familiar ring to it."

"That's what I thought."

Gomez's forehead furrowed. "How did you know about this? You Googling around and stumbled upon it?"

"No. Angie came across it and told me last night. I called

Beckham Township sheriff."

"Maybe we should go there and see things for ourselves," Gomez said. "Maybe we have the wrong guy."

Vikki's insides tightened. She'd forgotten about Dr. Murdoch. Did they have the wrong guy? Before she could tie herself into a knot, her phone rang. The caller ID said: B'ham Sheriff's Off.

"Mattsen."

"Detective Victoria Mattsen?"

"Yes." Vikki heard the expulsion of air from the other end of the phone. It sounded like relief.

"I'm Sheriff Alison Slater. I got your message. Do you think our cases are related? Because right now, it's a big puzzle to us."

Vikki put her excitement in check and steadied her voice. She told her about Paige Arden's death, how she'd been stabbed multiple times and strangled with her sock.

"We think she knew the perp. We have the boyfriend in custody. But he said he didn't do it." A moment passed. "Sheriff, are you there?"

"Yes, I'm here. Our victim was stabbed numerous times, all over the body, with a screwdriver. We recovered it, but no prints. She was raped in the backseat, strangled with her sock, then put in the trunk. Such savagery."

Vikki told her about what she'd found online in different parts of the country. "Have you talked to the next of kin? Did the victim travel for a photo shoot recently?"

"Yes, Brie's roommate said she did two days before the incident. Why?"

Vikki's pulse raced. "One more question before I answer that. Were there any peculiar smells around the victim?"

"Funny you should ask that. I was the first on the scene. When I opened the trunk, it smelled of blood and raspberries. But I didn't find any."

Vikki exhaled with a shudder. "It also smelled of raspberries around our victim," she said.

"Does that mean something?"

"Our ME said the smell is from a lubricant the perp used during the assault," Vikki said, remembering what Dr. Brandon had said. *Find a suspect with that in his glove compartment or toilet bag, and that narrows it down further.* "And she also had traveled for a photo shoot."

"In that case, this is probably the work of a serial killer," Sheriff Slater said. "I can't believe I have one in my town."

"Or maybe passing through," Vikki said under her breath.

"What was that?"

Vikki cleared her throat. "Did you get the name of the photo studio Brie visited?"

"I'm not sure. One second."

People talking in the background reached Vikki, but she couldn't determine what was said. Moments later, the sheriff came back.

"I asked the deputy who spoke with Brie's roommate. She did ask, but the roommate didn't know."

Vikki nodded. "Let's keep in touch. I'll see what I can find out about the photographer from my end. It can't be a coincidence that the two victims went for a photo shoot before they were murdered."

"I second that," Sheriff Slater said. "If we have any new information, I'll let you know."

They hung up.

"The smell of raspberry was there, too?" Gomez asked.

"And the vic also went for a photo shoot in New York." Vikki opened the murder folder on her desk and flipped through the pages. She found what she was looking for, picked up the phone, and dialed.

It was answered on the third ring. "Hello."

"Hi, Jessica. Detective Mattsen here. I need your help."

CHAPTER TWENTY-SIX

"Did he do it?" Jessica asked.

Vikki was torn. When in doubt, the truth shall set you free. "Jessica, I don't know. The evidence is there. The witness has lied already and is not credible. I've seen many cases that were not what it seemed." She took a breath. "But I know that we have a new promising lead."

"Not Kevin? I've already lost one friend—I don't want to lose another," Jessica said in a shaky voice.

"Not Kevin. That's why I need your help. Did Paige mention the name of the photographer she visited in New York?"

"Oh my God."

Rustling and a loud thud followed on the other end of the phone. "Jessica?"

"Sorry, I lost my grip on the phone. Yes, I know him. Donald Crimson. Are you sure? He's a well-known, sought-after photographer. I was supposed to go with Paige for the shoot but changed my mind. He was suggesting things I didn't want to do."

Vikki scribbled the name on the cover of the case file.

Her heartbeat raced like a plane about to take off. "Things like what?" She added DMV records and financials and pushed the file to Gomez.

Gomez gave one nod, took the folder, and was soon typing one finger at a time. His gaze traveled between the keyboard and the monitor.

Jessica continued. "He suggested many ways a pretty girl can make a living by modeling...for the right audience. Paige jumped on it." She took a moment. "It wasn't my thing. I only ventured into contests to support Paige. Becoming a beauty queen changed her. Now she was out of her shell. In college, she became a party girl."

That was the same thing Fiona had said. Vikki directed the conversation back to Donald Crimson. "When was the last time you heard from him?"

"Two days ago. He called to express his condolences about Paige."

Vikki pushed the phone tight against her ear. The same day Brie was murdered. Talk about hiding in plain sight.

"He said he had business in the area," Jessica said. And if he finished on time, he'd drop by."

Vikki stiffened. "He has your address?"

"Yes, we filled out a form to sign up for his services," Jessica said. "You think he killed Paige?"

"Two nights ago, a beauty pageant winner from Beckham Township was found murdered by the roadside."

Jessica gasped.

"The methods were similar to what happened to Paige," Vikki said. "She'd had photos taken a few days earlier, too." The more Vikki talked, the more she was convinced Jessica was a potential target. "Jessica, is there somewhere you can go? Like, leave the house until we figure out where Mr. Crimson is?"

"You think he'll come after me? I'm not pretty. I don't

think I'm his type. Moreover, my dad will protect me. He has a gun...he has a license, of course."

Vikki sighed. "Call me at this number or nine-one-one if there's an emergency. Where are you now?"

"I'm driving home from the grocery store. I want to surprise my parents with their favorite meal when they return from work."

"When you get home, stay indoors, and don't let anyone in. I'll send an officer to watch your house until we know where Mr. Crimson is."

"Okay." Jessica hung up.

Vikki took a deep breath and exhaled. Earlier, Gomez had walked away from his table. Now he was back with a bunch of papers.

"That's Donald Crimson," Gomez said. "Single, thirty-five, and lives in New York. He's a successful freelance photographer and works with many A-list celebrities and supermodels. He also works with local small-town beauty queens. It helps them with their portfolios and getting discovered."

Vikki reached for it. "Can I see?"

Gomez handed her one sheet of paper with a picture from a license. Black hair, square-jawed, blue eyes. This was one of the few license photos Vikki had seen with the owner not looking like a hostage.

"He was raised by a single mother, who was a...wait for it, a model, and a working girl. She would hand him over to babysitters and caregivers. Young Donald was exposed to abuse from these caregivers."

Vikki's face shot up.

Gomez continued. "At thirteen, he was arrested for shoplifting. A bigger kid, a neighbor his mother had left him with, dared him to do so. The frustrated shop owner called the police and pressed charges. He was taken to Juvenile Hall when they couldn't reach his mother. He spent the night, and probably things happened that traumatized him.

"She died when he was fourteen. Stabbed multiple times and strangled by a boyfriend. He entered the foster care system and bounced from family to family. Finally, a lovely family picked him. A fire broke out while Donald was away at college, and the family that took him in died."

Vikki massaged her temples. She saw where this was going. "He blamed his mother for all the atrocities that happened to him. But she's dead, and he can't punish her. His twisted mind came up with a plan. Murder, pretty girls, and women who reminded him of his mother."

"Excellent, Mattsen," Gomez said. He continued to type. He got up. "I printed some stuff."

Vikki's mind flashed back to when her friend, Alexis, and her dad had been murdered. It had made her angry. She'd been so mad that she'd wanted to become a vigilante. But she hadn't. Levin had convinced her to join the police force instead. Vikki could relate to the anger. She would find the people who did it and bring them to justice. It wouldn't be a twisted fantasy like what Crimson was doing, murdering innocent people.

Gomez's voice pulled her out of her reverie.

"He drives a white Tesla X. His financial statement shows he rented a car from St. Ives on Sunday and Morristown two days ago at Safety Car Rentals. On the same days, homicides occurred in St. Ives and Beckham Township. I've already put out an APB. This should be—"

Gomez paused and cocked his head.

Vikki tapped her lip with her finger.

Gomez grinned and said, "I know that look. What's the light bulb that went off in your head?"

"I think Mr. Crimson rented a car and left his car at the

car rental business. He murdered Paige. Came back, took his car, and left."

"He's a meticulous cleaner from what we saw at Paige's apartment," Gomez said.

Vikki nodded. "But, after fifty-four wounds, I don't see how he didn't get some of her blood on him. And I don't see how he didn't leave DNA in the car in which he left the crime scene."

"I'll talk to Levin for a warrant," Gomez said. "Brainstorm with him on which judge to approach."

"Good. I'll go to Safety Car Rentals and see what I can find. We must bring that vehicle in."

CHAPTER TWENTY-SEVEN

Vikki walked into Safety Car Rentals. Two empty tables and a counter with a man behind it made up the front office. Voices drifted in from the back.

"Hi, I'm Mike. How can I help you?" said a twentysomething-year-old man with a big smile.

Vikki flashed her badge.

The smile on the guy's face vanished.

"I'm Detective Victoria Mattsen, SIPD. Don't worry. I'm not here for you. I need to see a particular car."

"Most of our cars are out already, but I'll see what I can do. Which one?"

Vikki looked him straight in the face. "The car rented by Donald Crimson on Sunday the fourth," she said.

Mike straightened. He stroked his barely there goatee. "It's a black Nissan Rogue."

Vikki was surprised he didn't need to consult his computer. "You know it?"

He nodded and tapped the screen of his computer. "Yeah. I can get you another Rogue. That one has a smell."

"A smell?"

He let out a breath. "The guy said he bought a gallon of bleach, which leaked! Now the car smells like a swimming pool." He raised his hand and dropped it. "I cleaned the inside personally twice, and the smell is still there."

Vikki let out a heavy sigh. A bitter smile stretched her lips. Whatever evidence he'd left behind was probably destroyed. "Can I see it?"

Mike pursed his lips, shaking his head. "You know, I can get you a Jaguar E-PACE at a discount. At the same cost to you as the Rogue."

Vikki said, "No. I want that Rogue."

Mike clasped his hands together as if in prayer. "We left the doors and windows open to air it, and—"

"And it rained," Vikki said. "She remembered the rain Monday and sharing an umbrella with Gomez. "You know what, let me see it. The car was involved in a homicide, and you guys have made every attempt to get rid of the evidence."

"Homicide? Like murder?" The color left Mike's face.

Vikki nodded.

"Come on. I'll show you," Mike said.

He took Vikki to the back of the strip mall. A corner was designated for their vehicles. The car in question had all its doors open. Vikki shook her head, not believing what she was seeing. A defense lawyer would rip this apart. She heard the argument in her head. Anyone could have planted the evidence there.

Despite the obstacles that could come up, she still proceeded. The inside smelled of bleach and an odor like washed sneakers left to air dry but never did.

"Tada! Here it is," Mike said.

"Thank you."

Vikki walked back to her car. They needed some other way to connect Mr. Crimson to Paige's apartment. When he'd entered the vehicle after the murder, he must have pulled the seat belt to strap it on. Vikki paused. What if…?

She grabbed a pair of gloves from her glove compartment. Mike was about to return to the office, and she called him.

"Mike? Can you video me on your phone?"

Mike squinted. "What?"

"I'm going to check for evidence somewhere I didn't check before. I need you to capture it on video. Then send it to me."

"Okay." Mike brought his camera from his back pocket and pointed it at Vikki.

Vikki ran back to the Rogue. She put the gloves on. "Are you recording?"

Mike nodded.

She carefully pulled out the seat belt on the driver's side, holding the metal piece. A dark brownish color emerged as if the seat belt was deliberately coated with the stuff. Vikki wanted to dance and sing at the top of her voice.

"Is-is that blood?" Mike stammered. "Oh God, I'm-I'm going to be sick."

"Anything you do, don't drop that camera." Moments later, Vikki let the belt roll back in. She tossed her head back, closed her eyes, and laughed.

She took out her phone and called Gomez.

"Gomez."

"It's me. I found the car. Could you have CSU send a flatbed to Safety Car Rentals? Please bring the warrant if you have it."

CHAPTER TWENTY-EIGHT

Vikki waited until the Nissan Rogue was loaded onto the flatbed. She drove behind it to the PD. Forensic investigators took over. She went to the offices to brief Levin and write a report while waiting for the blood analysis.

"You think that's Paige Arden's blood on the seat belt?" Captain Levin said.

"Very likely, sir. I think Donald Crimson managed to leave the apartment undetected, then drive himself to the car rental company. He wiped the vehicle with bleach, dropped the key into the rental night box, and left. Since then, no one else has rented the car."

"Nice work, Mattsen. Keep me posted."

Vikki poured a cup of coffee from the break room and a granola bar from the vending machine. She sat at her desk and called Beckham Township sheriff. She shared the progress on the rental car.

The Beckham sheriff's office received the APB, too, and was looking for a white Tesla and a man fitting Crimson's description.

"The FBI called," Sheriff Slater said. "They want to visit

the scene where Brie's body was discovered. I hope they'll take over. They have the resources to give it the attention it deserves."

"Oh. Yes, you're right. That also confirms we have a serial killer on our hands."

They talked a little, then Vikki hung up.

Dennis Mallory, Chief of CSU for SIPD, approached, waving a piece of paper. He was impeccable in a gray suit and white shirt.

"This time, I have a piece of smoking saliva."

"What?" Vikki said.

"The DNA analysis on the condom wrapper finally came back. We ran it through CODIS (Combined DNA Index System) and got a hit."

"Who?" Vikki and Gomez asked at the same time. They sounded like hooting owls.

"Donald Crimson," Mallory said.

Vikki's phone buzzed—incoming text.

It was from Jessica Mills. Vikki's blood ran cold as she read the two-word text.

He's here.

CHAPTER TWENTY-NINE

Vikki packed her Explorer behind the white Tesla. They had rushed over with the strobe lights flashing but no siren. They didn't want to alert him and cause him to panic. She exited, and Gomez did the same from the front passenger side.

She walked past the white car, her heart hammering under her bullet vest. They'd opted to go in just the two of them. But backup was on the way.

Gomez knocked on the door. "SIPD! Open up!"

Nothing.

He banged louder with his fist. "Police! Open up." He glanced at Vikki.

She gave the nod, pulled her Glock, and held it in a two-handed grip.

Gomez, gun in hand, stepped back and kicked the door. It took a second kick before the lock gave way.

Vikki went in first. "Police! We are armed! Donald Crimson, come out with your hands up!"

The door opened into a small foyer. To their left was a sitting room.

Nobody was there.

To their right was the dining room. Empty. Adjacent to the entrance door was a staircase. Ahead of them was the family room.

Gomez cautiously stepped into the dining and scanned the area. "Clear."

Vikki stepped forward, cautious. Her finger was on the trigger. Any more pressure, and the Glock was ready to spit fire.

"This is the police!" Gomez said. "We are armed. Donald Crimson, we know you're in there. Show yourself with your hands up!"

A shot rang out.

A whimper followed it, then a thud as something heavy crashed to the floor.

Vikki crouched low. Her heart hammered as she approached the living room, gun extended in front of her. She peeped. Jessica stood in front of a male form lying on the floor. In her hand was a gun.

Vikki stepped forward. "Jessica, put down the gun." Her voice was loud and clear. Her gun was aimed at Jessica. She took another step toward her.

"He-he came after me," Jessica said.

"Jessica, we need you to lower the gun," Gomez said. He, too, had his gun pointed at her.

It seemed to take an eternity—Jessica lowered her gun. Her shoulders shook while she sobbed.

Vikki holstered her gun and approached Jessica. "It's all over. I'll take the gun now."

Jessica let her disarm her. She glanced at the man lying on the floor. It was the same man she'd seen on the documents hours ago.

Gomez checked the man's pulse. He looked up and shook his head. Donald Crimson was no more.

CHAPTER THIRTY

Vikki sat outside at Flame and Frost Restaurant (FFR), not far from the shores of Lake Hopatcong. Angie Baxter and Susie Mellon sat with her, enjoying the gentle breeze and working on their dinner.

Angie speared a piece of grilled chicken with her fork, pointed it at Vikki, and smiled. "What's the status with Dr. Brandon? Wait, don't answer that. When are you going to thank me?"

Vikki's eyes narrowed. "For what?"

Susie threw up her hands. "The status of Dr. Brandon sounds better. Thank you for what?"

"For helping SIPD." Angie took a bite.

Vikki smiled and shook her head. She inhaled and let it out through her mouth. "That was one hell of a case, though." Her voice was low. She turned to Susie. "Angie connected the dots and figured out we were dealing with a serial killer. She also notified me about a similar case in Beckham Township."

Vikki told her about the case, with Angie chiming in.

"It ended with Jessica shooting Donald Crimson when he came for her."

"Wow, scary stuff," Susie said. "What's going to happen to Jessica Mills?"

Vikki shrugged. "Nothing. "It was self-defense. Preparedness meeting opportunity—the definition of luck. Her father took her to the shooting range when she was younger. She hated it, but it saved her life."

Angie sipped her beer. "No crime is excusable, but people like Donald Crimson who murder for the fun of it…it's mind-boggling."

"I know," Vikki said. "It's a sickness." She had skeletons in her closet, too. Talking about Crimson's murders made her feel like a fraud. She pushed that thought to the back of her mind. "I spoke with one of the FBI profilers, and he showed me a file they had on him."

Angie leaned forward.

Vikki shot her a look. "I don't want this in your paper tomorrow."

"I cross my heart and hope to die if it appears in *St. Ives Examiner*."

"Okay, it goes back to his childhood."

Angie rolled her eyes. "Here we go again."

Vikki ignored her. "His mother was an aspiring model and single mother. She was absent most of the time. She handed him over to a babysitter if she had a gig or photo shoot. Most of the time, these were neighbors, friends, and sometimes kids barely older than him. That exposed him to all sorts of abuse—physical, verbal, sexual, and everything in between."

Susie massaged her neck. "My God."

Vikki nodded. "I felt goosebumps like this guy had a reason to do what he did. Sometimes, she'd leave him alone in the apartment for days, hungry and lonely. But." Vikki raised a finger. "She always came back and made it up to him. Buy him a toy. Cook his favorite meal, whatever made him feel better."

"Blame it on his childhood, right?" Angie said.

"Don't shoot the messenger," Vikki said. "I'm only telling you what was there. Anyway, one day his mother dies. Stabbed multiple times, then strangled by a boyfriend. Now he's all alone. This time she's not coming back. He's bounced from foster care to foster care. Abuse after abuse. But this time, no Mommy to make him feel better after whatever he went through. No reprieve. He blames his mother for abandoning him."

"Poor kid," Susie said.

"Eventually, he finds a good home and flourishes. He matures, grows physically, and becomes a man. Now, he can hold his own. But he's very angry with his mother, but she's dead. Then, he assaulted a woman who looked like his mother. Pretty, young, an aspiring model, and he felt good."

"So, in all these women, he's killing his mother over and over again?" Angie said, shaking her head. "Sick bastard."

Susie made the time-out sign. "Enough scary stuff. Now tell us about Dr. Brandon?"

Heat rushed to Vikki's cheeks. "Looks like we're back to square one."

The End

Prologue

Dan Starr wore faded blue jeans, loafers, and a black t-shirt embossed with 'Writer' in white text. He sat in this study surrounded by shelves filled with books, scripts, movies, and movie props from his past life.

A clown mannequin from his first movie script stood in a corner. A Shadow box with memorabilia from his movie, *Oxidant*, hung on the wall.

Movie posters and framed pictures with celebrities who wanted to capture eternity with the then twenty-two-year-old wonder boy dominated the remaining wall spaces.

"I'm a great fan of your work. Can I get a picture?" the actors used to say.

"You'll have a wall full of Oscars by the time you're forty!" said another.

The hits stopped as they'd started—without warning.

His executive producer days were far behind him. Today he taught English, creative writing, and drama at a high school. Sometimes sacrifices were necessary for self-preservation.

Dan swept a finger from right to left, turning the pages of the novel *Sambisa Escape* on his iPad. He leaned back in the chair and pondered the mass kidnapping of students. A school of all girls. Any chance of that happening in the school where he taught?

It could, but it would only be a matter of time before the perps were apprehended.

Dan Starr shut his eyes and inhaled. The flowery and fruity perfume from one of his last pupils, a little girl and her mother, still lingered in the air. The little girl loved to sing and act. But so did every other eight-year-old girl.

He didn't think she was special like her mother did. Like most life skills, the more you practice, the better you get at it. He wasn't going to tell anyone to move on. They should decide on their own. As long as he was getting paid, he'd continue to teach.

Most people took Sundays off to rest. To him, why waste the day? It was the day he took care of his special students.

The sudden blast of noise pulled him out of his thoughts. He glared at the wall between his study and the living room. It was the TV in the living room. A wall separated him from his wife. A muscle in his jaw twitched. Was she doing it on purpose?

Dan took a deep breath and let it out slowly. He'd almost fallen for her ploy. She'd planned to get him mad and drag him into a confrontation. He wouldn't fall for that.

He lifted his glass of brandy and took a deep drink. The fiery liquid burned as it traveled down, giving him a cozy feeling.

He'd cut off most of the noise and focused on the novel. Only the occasional creaking and groaning of the old home settling came through.

He returned to his reading, flipping from page to page as the adventure of the terrorists and schoolgirls unfolded. He lifted his head. Was that a creak? It must be the French windows. He'd opened them when one of his students arrived smelling of marijuana. Dan went back to his reading.

Thirty minutes later, the air got cooler. His skin broke out in goosebumps—time to shut the windows.

He took another sip from his glass, put the iPad down, walked over, and shut the window. The sound of croaking frogs and chirping insects disappeared.

"Good."

Shrill laughter came from the living room. Dan strolled over to the double glass doors between his study and the corridor and shut those, too. He went back to his chair and sat.

Something hard and cold pushed against the skin behind his ear. He whirled.

"What—"

Three things happened almost simultaneously—a loud noise. Searing pain like hot water poured into his ear, followed by darkness.

Chapter 1

"All right, Vikki, Susie's here!" Angie said. "You can ask her about her welfare. Is Susie okay? Is she having trouble at home?" She gestured at Susie with both hands. "Go, Vikki. She's yours."

Susie, sitting opposite Angie, batted her eyelids and smiled. "Shut up, Angie!"

It was girls' night out—Vikki with Angie and their friend, Susie, a transplant from Rhode Island. Vikki wore blue jeans and a button-down white shirt, untucked to hide her holster. She'd draped her light jacket over the back of her chair. But she felt like she was sitting close to a fire roasting marshmallows. Angie had put her on the spot. All she'd done was ask after Susie, who was on the run from a domestic situation. Was it a crime to ask after your friends?

The waiter saved her, appearing at the right moment with their appetizers.

"Excuse me," the waiter said. She moved their glasses and drinks to the side and laid down a platter of beef nachos supreme. Next came a basket of wings in barbecue sauce with a blue cheese dip.

"Nice," Angie said. She reached for the platter and pulled off a nacho loaded with beef, a slice of jalapeño, and cheese.

Angie Baxter and Vikki had become fast friends after Vikki had moved to St. Ives some years ago. Vikki shared information with Angie about cases now and then. She wrote for *St. Ives Examiner*, and sometimes, Vikki picked her brain for research and, in return would provide information for her newspaper before anyone else.

Vikki pushed around the rocks in her Henny and Coke with the red straw. She cocked her head and said, "It's the cop in me. Sometimes it's on autopilot." She raised both hands in surrender. "I'm going to stop asking. If something happens to her, you are to blame." She pointed at Angie.

"Hello?" Susie said. "You guys are talking about me as if I'm not here." She turned to Vikki. "Thanks so much for your concern. Don't mind Angie. It's not that type of domestic situation, more of...[click here for next in series]